THE HOSTAGE

PETER O'MAHONEY

THE HOSTAGE:
A GRIPPING CRIME MYSTERY
Jack Valentine Book 2

Peter O'Mahoney

Copyright © 2020
Published by Roam Free Publishing.
peteromahoney.com

1st edition.

Cover design by Belu.
https://belu.design

ALSO BY PETER O'MAHONEY

In the Jack Valentine Mystery Series:

Gates of Power
The Shooter
The Thief
The Witness

*****

In the Tex Hunter Legal Thriller series:

Power and Justice
Faith and Justice
Corrupt Justice
Deadly Justice
Saving Justice
Natural Justice
Freedom and Justice
Losing Justice
Failing Justice

*****

In the Joe Hennessy Legal Thriller series:

The Southern Lawyer
The Southern Criminal
The Southern Killer

THE HOSTAGE

JACK VALENTINE MYSTERY BOOK 2

PETER O'MAHONEY

CHAPTER 1

AT LEAST twenty-five smiling children were on the play equipment, at least twenty-five potential kidnapping targets.

They looked so happy, so carefree, and so innocent on the Saturday morning. For most of the parents at the playground it was a normal start to the weekend, a moment to let their hair down after another stressful week at work. A chance to forget the stress, forget the rush, and forget the anxiety. Let their kids be kids, and take in some time outside.

The air was fresh. It was a bright spring morning, and although the sun had been up for two hours, dew still clung to the grass. Some of the children wore warm coats, others were comfortable in only their t-shirts. It was a colorful array, matching the spring flowers just emerging around the edges of the park. This was a place of happiness, of innocent joy and beauty, but danger lurked there too.

The kidnapper had parked on the road near the edge of the playground, only twenty yards away from the bottom of the slide. The kidnapper searched for the right target, scanning over the boys and girls, laughing freely with no idea of how easy their lives were.

They were rich kids, privileged and comfortable, the sons and daughters of people with money.

But the children didn't know that yet, they were still so happy. So free.

The glee in their voices, the excitement on their faces.

Their clothes were so pristine, so perfect. For them, life was still an easy collection of days spent with friends; learning, laughing, growing. They knew danger was alive in their city of Chicago, they had practiced school shooting drills earlier that week, but it was just part of their routine, and always an arm's length away. Their schools were well protected, with very visible security, so real danger was still an abstract concept. Until now. Not one of the children sensed the threat. They were completely unaware of the menace lurking in the street.

The kidnapper spotted the perfect target.

The father looked distracted, he looked like he wanted to be somewhere else. Clean-cut and well-dressed, it was clear this was anything but a day off for him. This man didn't have days off. Time spent with his child was more an obligation than a joy, a task that had to be negotiated and carried out, while business went on as usual. He took a phone call, shooing his beautiful daughter away. The father couldn't ignore his phone; the kidnapper knew that. The phone was the father's lifeblood, his way to make more money. The father was only ever concerned with his wealth. It was his driving force, his reason for getting up in the morning, his all-consuming motivating factor. What he really lived and breathed for.

The phone conversation became louder, and the father stepped away from the playground, away from his five-year-old blonde daughter, putting her in imminent and growing danger with every fateful step he took, both father and daughter completely unaware of the kidnapper's eyes fixated on them now, watching their every move.

There were so many choices, so many distracted parents. This Saturday morning was a smorgasbord of options.

One five-year-old child had even wandered away from the play equipment by himself, completely ignoring his parents, following a small bird. His wonder was admirable, although they say that curiosity killed the cat.

Kids are so gullible, so easily convinced.

All the kidnapper needed was an instant, one fleeting second of opportunity.

Noble looking, gently swaying, poplar trees lined the yard around the play equipment, and the grass was recently cut. A dog park was next door, and the yapping of the dogs only raised the level of joy in the area. There was a sense of innocence, a sense of joyous freedom.

The kidnapper stepped out of the van and walked closer to the playground, careful not to draw any attention. The kidnapper had dressed to fit in, to look the part of a parent in the upscale suburb, clothes stylish and expensive, but not flashy, clearly designer but without any obvious labels.

"Hello." The kidnapper leaned down to one little girl, resting a knee on the ground. "I have some chocolates for you."

The girl smiled.

She was a happy girl, blue eyes, still carefree, a look of pure innocence. Her skin was soft, her cheeks round, and her clothes were clearly brand new. Her shoes were perfectly white Mary Janes, her socks pulled up to her knees, and her fingernails looked like they had been manicured.

The girl didn't have a worry in the world. Not yet.

"I love chocolates." The girl smiled.

The plan was perfect. So simple. So easy.

Closer.

The other parents in the park were so at ease, so calm, that they didn't realize the danger lurking within their own park. They were distracted, too busy with their own lives, their own worlds, to keep their offspring safe.

The kidnapper was an opportunist, a person ready to take advantage of the distracted.

The blonde girl's father had walked across the road, yelling loudly on the phone. His conversation had become more animated, more intense, and he didn't want the children to hear the words that he was going to use. The father was dressed in a polo shirt, chino shorts, and loafers; all brand new. His watch looked expensive, and his slicked back hair looked like it was conditioned only with the best that money could buy.

The kidnapper knew the children at the playground in Lincoln Park, Chicago, would be the offspring of the wealthy. These were the children that had the latest gadgets, the newest toys, and the finest clothes. These children were likely never to want for anything, except the attention of their parents. And money couldn't buy that.

The kidnapper was there to teach the parents that lesson; to teach them that time with children is fleeting, it's gone too quickly. Life is brief. And the best way to teach someone to appreciate what they have, is to take it away.

One of the mothers stepped past the kidnapper, pushing her child in a stroller, and, to her credit, she hesitated with a momentary look of suspicion. The kidnapper almost wished the mother would say something, would try to stop them, to do anything to prevent them from doing what they were about to do.

But she didn't.

Her baby gurgled, and with obvious relief, she

bent forward to fuss with its blanket and continued on.

Her fear of social reprisal, of making a scene and drawing unwanted attention was stronger than her fear of suspicion.

The kidnapper knew there was nothing to stop them from what they were going to do now.

It was the only way. The wheels had been set in motion and there was no turning back.

"I have chocolates in my van." The kidnapper smiled and pointed to the white van parked close by. "I have boxes and boxes of chocolate."

The blonde girl looked over to her father, still talking loudly on the phone, his actions exaggerated, his anger clear. She was scared of her father's anger.

She took the kidnapper's hand, skipping as he led her to the van. She was chattering nonsense the way small children do.

Closer now.

The kidnapper opened the back door. It creaked loudly but no one looked.

The kidnapper pointed to the boxes of chocolates, and then checked for any suspicious eyes watching them.

No one. No one had even looked twice. Shame on them. The blonde girl stepped into the van, drawn to the chocolates. And the kidnapper quietly closed the van door.

The plan had begun.

CHAPTER 2

I HATE the news.

It's always filled with so much despair, so much anger, and there's so much focus on the worst that life has to offer. Murders, terror attacks, arson—crime is so commonplace that the facts blend into the background, barely raising an eyebrow. We become calloused by default, toughened and hardened to it all as a matter of self-preservation. If not, we'd be nervous wrecks from all the negativity bombarding us on the screen. But there's one type of story that always breaks through, that always registers no matter how calloused to the world people become—anything to do with innocent children. And so it was today in my favorite bar, a story that killed all conversation.

The screen above the bar was playing the headline news and it was running with the story that a third child had been kidnapped in the last three days in Florida. The sunny streets of Florida were a long way from the cold of Chicago, but I felt the parents' pain. They were crying on the television, unable to hold back their fear, anguish, and despair. Every parent's worst nightmare. They dropped the ransom, dropped the bag stuffed full of money in the park, just like they were instructed, but the kidnapper ran away with the child once the FBI showed up. They were making a public plea to the kidnappers when the bartender turned up the television. Please, oh please, return our child unharmed, they cried. I didn't hold out much hope that that would happen, and by the sounds of the parents' cries, they knew it too.

"The worst thing about these stories," the man in a dark green flannel shirt next to me said. "Is the copycats it spawns. These people think they can get away with it now. All of a sudden kidnapping is a simple way to make a quick million dollars." He pointed at the television. "If people see it working, it suddenly becomes a viable business plan."

The bartender grunted his response, while I went back to my drink.

When I said this place was my favorite bar, I wasn't talking about a trendy new-age hipster joint with fancy names for cocktails and craft beer that tasted like fruit juice. Nope. The Angry Friar was a place where the bathrooms were vandalized—and rarely fixed—the floor was sticky, and the beer tasted like wholesome dirty goodness. The type of place where blood stained the edge of the pool table and nobody bothered to clean it off, where the lighting was dim enough not to notice the food stains on the tables, and the door was shut no matter the weather to prevent any hint of daylight coming through.

In short, the type of place I felt comfortable.

"I could never harm a kid," the guy two bar stools down added. His knuckles were scabbed, the tattoos ran up his neck, and he was missing a few front teeth. "You could never pay me enough to do that to some innocent little soul."

I understood the parents' pain on the television, I understood how much anguish they must've been experiencing. I knew what loss was, I'd swum in a sea of it for years, often to the point of drowning. I always dreamed of having a child with my late wife Claire, may she rest in peace. I thought that a little girl would've been perfect, perhaps I would've named her Snow, Summer, or Winter. Something memorable for what would've been a memorable girl. But that would never happen now.

We had a niece, Alannah, that we both adored. She was a sweet little girl who was obsessed with butterflies, anything to do with butterflies. She loved watching them with the keen eye of a young biologist and would dance around with a look of sheer joy on her face as she followed their erratic flutterings. Her room was covered in pictures of butterflies too, as was her favorite clothing, and she would draw and paint them all the time, in vivid, wondrous colors, like they were magical beings. That's what we always got her for her birthdays, something to do with her beloved butterflies. She would be nine years old by now. I hadn't seen her in a while. When my Claire passed away, she left a hundred thousand dollars behind in her will for little Alannah. We always thought we would be right there, watching her and our own child grow up, cousins playing together, having a shared early history. But life doesn't always work out the way you think it will or hope it does. The money was Claire's way of wishing her the best for the future.

The grimy and fading mirror behind the bar alerted me to something unusual behind me—someone that looked like they could drink the best whiskey and even afford to pay for it, not that there was any of it here. The man behind me, seated at a table by himself, was swirling his drink, occasionally looking up at me, or at least the back of my head. He was dressed in a canary yellow polo shirt, slacks and shiny shoes. His arms were tanned a deep walnut brown, probably from spending too long sailing his yacht on the weekends, although his left wrist was marked by a stark band of white. At least he had the good sense to take off his expensive watch before he came into a dive bar like this—so the guy had some smarts, but that didn't mean he was clever, only cautious and apprehensive. But not cautious enough.

I wasn't the only person whose attention was being drawn by this stranger, with some of the locals staring his way too, perhaps wondering if he was a cop or not. I didn't believe that for a second. He wasn't disguised enough for a cop and his clothes clearly cost too much money; undercover cops made the effort to blend in, although all too often badly, at least to the trained eye like mine. One of the guys playing pool approached the man with slicked back hair, and asked him, politely of course, if he had a problem.

The man didn't respond, not even looking up from his drink, he just stared at it fixated. It was a brave move, but he had the resolve to ignore his inquisitor, as if he were insignificant and didn't even warrant an acknowledgement or reply. The pool player soon lost interest, shrugged his shoulders and left him to it, and he went back to the table, missing his next shot badly.

A moment later the man looked up from his drink, eyes focused once again on me. This time I turned from the mirror and looked him squarely in the eye, not with menace but a look, firm and uncompromising, that begged a simple question: You need something, stranger? He quickly diverted his eyes from me. If I didn't know better, I'd say he was working up the courage to hit on me.

I left my drink, although there was still a mouthful of my Goose Island IPA remaining, dropped some bills on the counter for the bartender, and walked towards the door. When I reached it, I glanced behind me, and saw the man had made a move.

Now it was time for me to make mine.

I stepped outside, surprised to see that the sun had already disappeared for the day, dusk was upon us and a chill hung heavy in the air. Here I waited. Down the bottom of a short flight of stairs from an overpass, our dive bar was usually hidden from the tourists, the wanderers, or the office workers. If you didn't know The Angry Friar was there, you'd never notice it. There was no big flashy sign enticing you in, no advertising boards and certainly no outdoor seating.

It was just the way we liked it.

Nobody wanted new comers; not the owner, not the bartender, and certainly not the clientele.

The door opened again and my hand went straight to the man's throat—always a favorite move.

The benefit of being six-foot-four and broad shouldered was that most people talked when I threatened them. I slammed my new friend against the brickwork, hard enough for his head to bounce off the wall, and brought my nose to his, the aroma of his expensive cologne mingling with another unmistakable smell: fear. His eyes widened as a look of panic spread rapidly across his face. Whatever he had been hoping to achieve, it certainly wasn't this. I didn't grip him especially hard, at least for me, but he still gasped for air, sucking it in rapid little bursts, half due to his semi contracted windpipe, half out of abject terror. This was not a man used to physical altercations, whereas for me it was just another day in the office.

"You've got five seconds to tell me what you

want."

Pretty-boy tried to say something, but clearly my knuckles were too far into his throat. I loosened my pressure, but not enough for him to wriggle free.

"You're Jack Valentine, the private investigator?" he said, rasping.

"I am."

"My daughter's been kidnapped." There was a tear in his eye. "And I need your help."

CHAPTER 3

SOMETIMES, POSH is an understatement. The penthouse apartment of Chase Martin was enormous, sitting on top of a high-rise in the upscale suburb of the Gold Coast. On one side the vista from the floor to ceiling windows stretched far out onto Lake Michigan, and on the other, a spectacular view of Downtown Chicago, the architecturally designed buildings shining in all their glory. The kitchen was decked out in all the latest top-brand gadgets, but it was pretty obvious they got very little use, Chase Martin was not the kind of man to make his own coffee, let alone cook his own dinner. The shiny mixer, blender, espresso machine, grinder, and juicer were all for show, not function. As for furniture, the minimalist white leather couch looked pristine, as though it was hardly ever sat on, leaving me to wonder where his daughter played when she stayed over. No doubt she spent plenty of time parked in front of the TV or iPad. The expensive show home and her father's rich lifestyle were not to be disturbed by a child's natural need for play and mess.

Clearly, Chase Martin tried his best to dress down

when he came into the bar.

Even though it was approaching 8pm, my assistant Casey May arrived not long after I called her, only a few moments after we arrived at Chase Martin's apartment. Casey was always on call, always ready to take the message, always ready to spring into action. Blonde, smart, sexy; her smooth demeanor was the perfect foil to my gruff.

"Can I offer you a drink?" Chase gestured to a well-stocked upscale liquor display. "I'm not sure I have your drink of choice though Jack, I'm afraid," he added with an ever so slight snobbish condescension.

Sensing my disgust at the flashy display of wealth, Casey jumped in and answered for both of us.

"No thanks, we'd rather just get on with it."

That was my cue.

"So why us, and why not the cops?"

"I couldn't go to the cops, not after what happened in Florida. I couldn't risk it. And the cops around here are as incompetent as they come. And the FBI... well, I've already had a few run-ins with the FBI with my business, and I wouldn't trust them not to bungle it like they did down south. It's not worth the risk."

"So you came looking for a private investigator."

"I've spent the whole day trying to think of what to do. Trying to see if I knew anything before I got someone else involved. I've looked at every option and every opportunity, and this is where I'm at. I

don't want anything bad to happen to my daughter."
He shook his head. "I researched the best investigator
in Chicago and your name kept coming up, but I
couldn't call you. I'm scared that my phone is bugged,
and they're looking at my internet searches. I had to
come see you in person."

Holding his phone, a modern piece of technology
if there ever was one, I read the message:

*****

I have your daughter. I need one million in cash.
In a bag. You have five days. I'll contact you with the
drop point. No cops involved or your daughter gets
hurt. You're being watched.

*****

"It's short and sweet. To the point," Casey said.
"They haven't given anything away from their
language."

"It's someone you know," I said to Chase. I stood
at the window, apparently looking out at the view but
watching for Chase's reaction in the reflection, hands
behind my back. "And they know your daughter."

He was definitely surprised by that. "What makes
you say that?"

"Five days is too long for a typical kidnapping.
Usually, a kidnapper needs the transaction over and

done with as quick as possible. If you say that you can't get the money in that time, then they'll give you an extension, but they don't need it to drag on. The longer it goes, the more likely the cops would put together a good team. So what that message says to me is that they know your daughter and are comfortable looking after her for five days."

"Or they're good with kids," Casey added.

"Perhaps," I responded. Casey liked to keep an open mind, I preferred to follow my instincts. "They're not panicking anyway, and they also know that you have the money to deliver."

"I've heard that you're the best." Chase smiled. "That's why I came looking for you."

"This isn't a time for smiles." I grunted my response.

"Yes." He nodded. "Sir. Sorry."

I was often called Sir, not because of my fashion— black t-shirt, leather jacket, jeans and boots— but usually for my size, as an attempt to appease my character. I'd never wanted to be a real Sir, knighted by that there queen they had over in London, England; but hey, I'll take it.

"Talk us through the whole day." I came back to sit on the white leather couch. It was more comfortable than my bed and probably cost ten times as much. "Tell us what happened."

"I took Millie, my five-year-old daughter, to Lincoln Park at 9:30 on Saturday morning. I—"

"Is that your usual routine?" Casey interrupted, taking notes on her electronic tablet.

"It is. That's what we do every Saturday morning. I share custody of Millie with Tanya, my ex-wife, and I pick her up on Saturday morning, and drop her back to her mom's on Sunday night. We always start the weekend with a play at the park, and then an ice-cream. Her Mom's pretty strict on sugar, actually she's obsessed with it, says nonsense like it's pure white and deadly, but I don't believe that claptrap, so it's our special treat."

"And she just vanished from the park, right under your nose?"

"No." He looked down. It was the first time I saw him look embarrassed. "I was on the phone, taking a work call. Millie was playing and there were probably around ten or so other people in the park. I stepped away from the playground as the conversation got heated, I didn't want to disturb the other people, or to worry Millie. The call went on longer than I expected..." Chase trailed off. Pausing to collect himself he continued, "After ten minutes I came back. And Millie was gone."

"You didn't check on her for ten minutes?" Casey questioned.

"It was an important call." He shrugged. "There were so many other people around, I thought she would've been fine. I never expected this. Not in Lincoln Park. Not at a busy play area."

"And nobody saw anything?"

"Not a thing. I was panicking, asking everyone there if they'd seen anything, and then this text comes through about five minutes after I realize she's gone. It was when I knew that she hadn't just wandered off."

I'd dealt with a kidnapping once before. The parents contacted me when their child didn't come home from school, and they received a ransom note, stating no police and a five-thousand-dollar ransom. The problem was, the ransom note contained the watermark from a local cake-making business. I pretended I was a customer, busted the place up, and found the child watching television in the back. It was an Aunty who wanted money from the wealthier part of their family. I took some cake—Boston Cream Pie, my favorite, and it was pretty good too—returned the kid, and told them to behave in the future. Nothing like finances to fire up a long-running family drama.

"Will Tanya get suspicious if you don't return Millie on Sunday?"

"This week, Tanya asked if I could have Millie for an extra couple of days so she could pick up a few more shifts at the bar she works at. Apparently, money is a bit tight for her at the moment and she was desperate to pick up some extra cash. She won't even know that Millie is missing. If she calls, I'll say that Millie is busy."

Casey and I exchanged a knowing look as Chase grabbed his phone, providing his ex-wife's contact and address details.

"She works at a bar, is tight for money, and you live here?" Casey raised her eyebrows.

"We signed a pre-nup before we got married."

"How romantic."

"It was on the advice of my lawyer. He could see that it wasn't going to last, and I knew it as well, but she got pregnant, so we got married. Millie's only five, but we divorced three years ago." Chase shrugged. "I was right—it didn't last long. The pre-nup was the right thing to protect my wealth."

"And Millie spends most of her time with Tanya?"

"I pay alimony but Tanya is legally required to use it for Millie, if she wants extra spending money, Tanya has to earn it herself. I'm not a charity, and I don't believe in hand outs. I've pulled myself up, done it the hard way, that's how character is built, through struggle. In the long run I'd be doing her a disservice, not a favor, by dropping money in her lap."

"Uh-huh," Casey replied disinterestedly.

"New wife or girlfriend?" I asked.

"I have a new girlfriend. Ruby Jones. She's an Instagrammer." He smirked. "Only twenty-five. Dumb as a log, but hot. So damn hot. She has the body of an angel."

"Romance isn't dead," I said. "And do you know where Ruby was when Millie disappeared?"

"Ruby?" Chase looked faintly amused by the idea. "Well, she stayed overnight but I left her here when I went to pick up Millie. She was still asleep when I left and playdates at the park aren't really Ruby's thing. She's more of an indoor play sort of girl, if you get my meaning."

I managed to ignore his wink, but I noticed Casey couldn't quite stifle her grimace. For the sake of Millie and the case I decided to change gears again.

"Tell me more about Tanya's connections. Are you still in contact with any of her relatives?"

"Damon Hardy, that's Millie's grandfather, Tanya's father. Tanya and I didn't separate on good terms, but Damon has stayed in my life. I think he secretly hopes we'll get back together for Millie's sake, you know." He rolled his eyes, then suddenly became more serious. "He's a good guy though," he said, nodding his head with a sigh. "He's got cancer, and won't live much longer, so he needs to spend as much time with Millie as possible. The rest of the family doesn't speak to me."

"New partner for Tanya?"

"Kyle Waters. Ex-army. Tough exterior, looks mean, and not the brightest guy around. We get along okay when we have to. He drives trucks now that he's not in the army. I'm not sure he's smart enough to get a real job."

Chase handed a picture of Millie across to me— blonde, blue eyes, gorgeous smile. An angel if there ever was one. I passed the photo to Casey.

"Any idea who would do this? Anyone in mind?" Casey continued.

"I don't think my ex-wife would do it. And I don't think her family would've done it, but there's one group of people that immediately came to mind." He drew a long breath and ran his hand through his hair. "I'm an investment broker, and this one group of investors lost a million dollars five months ago. That's what my first thought about this was. They've been chasing me for the investment the last five months, but the money was lost and there was nothing I could do."

"How was the money lost?"

"In an investment gone bad. It was supposed to be a simple transaction into a start-up company that was going to challenge the way buses operate. They were designing an app that let the user track the bus, call for it to come to their door if on a main road, or make it wait up to a minute while the user ran to it. We were going to triple the money once the company went public. Almost guaranteed. But the company folded and declared bankruptcy as soon as the million-dollar investment went in." He shrugged as though this was no big deal.

"However," I sat back on the couch. "I bet that you still took a commission. Say five percent."

"Ten percent." He smiled proudly. "A hundred thousand in commission."

"So even though you lost all their money in an investment," Casey raised her eyebrows. "You still made a hefty return?"

"That's the game we play." He smiled again, hands opened wide. "It was all above board. I did nothing illegal. And there was no recourse against the company, because it was based overseas."

Casey could barely hide her disgust.

"Legal is not the same as moral."

"It's the game. Money's a game. Life's a game. Everything is a game." He reiterated. "And listen, I'll pay you one-hundred-thousand if you can find my daughter before the money drop. If not, I'll pay you fifty thousand to make sure the drop goes well. But we can't get the FBI or the cops involved. No one but us is to find out. I can't have the FBI searching my apartment."

"Just another game," Casey muttered under her breath so that only I could hear.

I grunted in response.

"I'm going to need a list of the investors and anything else you think might be relevant."

"Because it was an open investment, the list is publicly available," he responded calmly as he opened his laptop. "Anyone could access the list of investors and their names."

I walked across to the bookshelf, and picked up another picture of Millie—happy, smiling, and carefree, wearing a dress with several big colorful

29

pineapples printed on it.

"Alright if I take this?" I asked.

Chase shrugged, "Sure."

Even though I'd only just met him, I didn't like Chase Martin, not one bit. I didn't like the way his hair was slicked back, I didn't like his arrogant smugness, and I didn't even like the look of his long horse-like face.

But I would do everything to save Millie Martin. We only had five days, and I was going to have to act fast, real fast. If I didn't, well, the consequences didn't bear thinking about.

CHAPTER 4

AS THE clock ticked past midnight, Casey and I left the penthouse, descending to the chilled streets of Chicago below.

It was refreshing to be back in gritty reality after the sterile sanctuary of Chase's apartment. Everything up there was so false, a contrived pretty picture of the world that bore little semblance to the truth.

The street outside the apartment building in the Gold Coast was unusually quiet, but it was the early hours on a Sunday morning. I looked around to see if I could see anyone watching us, any hint that someone had eyes on Chase's place, but I didn't see anything unusual, apart from a drunken fool trying to sleep in the middle of the road. I walked across, gave him a gentle push with my foot, and he snapped awake, confused about where he was. Casey and I helped him to his feet, and he made it across the rest of the road before falling back down. The gutter was a better place to sleep than the road.

I considered that my good deed for the day, almost like we were guardian angels for the drunken fools of the world. There was no shortage of them in this city,

31

but I could empathize, I'd spent my fair share of time with the bottle.

Despite our good deed, Casey and I were silent until we were in my Chevy truck, doors closed and locked, and no one else around. I checked over my shoulder looking for anything unusual, then the mirrors to see any movements. Nothing.

I took a deep breath, allowing the familiar smell of my truck to focus my mind. I spent so much time in my truck, it was like a second home.

"Thoughts?" Casey opened her tablet to review her notes.

"It's someone that knows Chase and his routine. They've probably been monitoring it for weeks to find out that he goes to the playground with his daughter on a Saturday morning. Or maybe they were already familiar with it." I started the engine and turned on the heater. "And there were no screams or any struggle. Nobody saw anything unusual, and there was no fuss. Millie wasn't forced to go anywhere or do anything. She went willingly."

Casey nodded then punched some more details into her tablet, quickly pulling up the information she was after.

"Ok. Ruby Jones—the Instagrammer. Twenty-five. Tall, pretty, redhead." Casey scrolled through the details. "Describes herself on social media as an 'influencer.'"

"One of those," I groaned. "Someone who tries to

influence others through social media so that they can feel good about themselves.""

"Exactly right. She has literally hundreds of photos of her and Chase in the past year, but none with Millie." Casey opened another page on the publicly available social media profiles of Ruby Jones. "Oh, interesting; her last post, posted at 9:15am on Saturday, is a picture of her with the view from Chase's apartment in the background, and she has written: 'Excited about this fresh, new start.'"

"What does that mean?"

"Everything these influencers do is cryptic. It's designed to get you asking questions, make you want to know more. She's baiting people to ask questions, but she hasn't answered them." Casey bit her bottom lip. "Perhaps she's talking about a fresh start without Millie. She clearly doesn't like the girl."

"What makes you say that?"

"Well," Casey said, scanning the page, mentally collating the information and sorting it into a single thought. "Not only are there no pictures of Millie, but she uses the hashtag '#kidfreeandlovingit' a lot."

"Subtle."

"Indeed. And she has a few posts and comments about dropping friends who settle down and start families. 'Boring' apparently."

I nodded and ran my hands around the smooth steering wheel of my Chevy. The sensation helped focus my mind.

I did a lot of thinking in my Chevy. It was almost a mobile office for me, especially when time was of the essence, and the pressure was on. When the constant thoughts running through my head got to be too much, I would often jump in the driver's seat, turn up the tunes, and drive a hundred miles. That's when an idea would often leap into my head, a thought that had been brewing could come to the surface and get worked out.

"With social media," I turned to Casey. "Can you see what's posted at a particular location?"

"Anything that's publicly available, yes."

"Look at the park, anything that's posted around 9:30am on Saturday."

Casey spent a few moments scrolling through the photos before turning the tablet to me.

"Here, look at this. This mother posted a photo of her child on the swing at 9:33am and in the background you can see Chase on the phone." She pointed at the tablet. "But no Millie."

"He's a long way from the playground."

"Not great parenting," Casey added. "And this post, it's from another mother at 9:36am. That looks like Millie playing on the slide behind her son."

"It is Millie." I confirmed. "Anyone else in the picture?"

"Not that I can see. I can do a broader search for the area, but that'll take some time to go through. According to the maps, there's a green space next to the playground, a row of shops across the road, and a parking lot nearby. I can use all those locations to see what we can gather on social media."

"Brilliant. In the morning, I'll also get you to check for any video surveillance footage from those shops," I added.

I tapped my hand on the door. I had to replace the door when someone ran into me during a previous job. The woman blindsided me, running a red light, but luckily no one was hurt. Not me, and apart from a few scratches, my beautiful Chevy made it through. I'd only had it a few months, an upgrade after destroying my last Chevy, a far older model, when I had to gain access to a private property by smashing through some wrought iron gates at high speed. Messy job.

"We can't do much now, so let's crash, get a few hours' sleep, and get back into it in the morning." Casey yawned. "We'll see things clearer in the morning, but we've only got five days, so what's the plan?"

"We've got two things to do—see if we can find Millie, and if we can't, prepare for a safe drop. We've got to prepare for a safe drop now, while trying to find her. We don't have much time, so it's our backup. We have to be prepared to save the girl's life with a ransom exchange."

The safe drop was not the way I wanted things to go, but the preliminary plans for it had to be made and quickly, getting ahold of that much cash was neither simple nor routine. After all, a million dollars was one hell of a lot of money to withdraw, it could raise serious suspicions on behalf of the bank, but Chase had given us his word that he could get it. For now, that was up to him, the financial world was his forte not mine, and what's more I didn't have time to follow or guide him through the process, after all, more pressing matters were at hand. But if the drop had to occur, I needed to be there, on site, hidden but watching and waiting with Casey, while Chase himself did the handover. That would be the tricky bit. The details of this were, as of yet, left unstated by the kidnapper, but hopefully they'd make a mistake, not a mistake that would harm Millie, but one that would let us nab them once Millie was safe and well.

Casey pulled a piece of paper from her handbag, amongst the files that were provided by Chase. He was co-operative, at least. Not likable, but then that's not a part of my job. My job isn't to make friends, it's to investigate, to peel the onion, so to speak, to see the multiple layers underneath the surface and see into the heart of the matter.

With the news on the television about the kidnapping gone wrong in Florida, I understood Chase's apprehension to have the police or FBI involved. It was too much of a risk. And I'd seen them blunder their way through plenty of investigations in the past. There were some good cops out there, but I'd met my fair share of incompetent ones too.

Casey's phone pinged: It was a message from Chase, he had already begun making arrangements to have the money available.

"Well, that's something," I said. "I wonder what on earth he told the bank. If that's where he went, it wouldn't surprise me if man like that had a ditch kit."

"Ditch kit?"

"Yeah, a safety deposit box with all the necessities in case he has to do a runner: gold, cash, passports, you know, that sort of thing."

Casey nodded. "How about this list of ten people that invested in his latest bankrupt venture? It seems a bit coincidental that they're asking for the same amount that was lost."

She had a point, but having said that, a million dollars was a nice round figure too, both to ask for and to count, after all, a kidnapper wouldn't ask for nine hundred and fifty-five thousand dollars.

Casey handed across a printout of the names.

"And look at this," said Casey. "It's the ex-wife's new boyfriend on the list."

"Interesting that his ex-wife's new boyfriend is on there and that Chase didn't mention it. The list is a good starting point; can you get me some background on all these names by the morning?" I glanced over the names of the poor souls who lost one hundred thousand each to that smug investment broker. And then my heart sunk. "Oh no."

"What's wrong?"

"I know one of the names on that list. A cop, a guy on the edge, and my late wife's brother." I put the Chevy into gear. "And he's going to be my first call tomorrow morning."

CHAPTER 5

SUNDAY MORNINGS are regarded as sacred, a moment to disappear from the world, forgetting about all the heavyweight worries, all the stresses of work, and all the troubles of the week. Thoughts of finances, worries about family, and fears of ill health are usually forgotten on long mornings in a warm bed, a chance to recover and revive. Usually, Sunday mornings are spent holding a loved one close, their warm body creating a sense of comfort and escape. A long breakfast, a quiet cup of coffee, and a nice read of the paper usually follows.

Usually.

Not this Sunday morning. Not when the life of a five-year-old girl was on the line. Not with just four days to go. And counting.

After a number of unsuccessful attempts at reaching him by phone, my brother-in-law, Ben Glazier, finally answered on the fifth try.

"Jack, it's 5am on Sunday morning." He moaned. "What do you want?"

"I don't have time to mess around." I was blunt. "I'm outside your front door."

"You're what?!"

He muttered an expletive then the phone hung up, and after a few moments, I heard the movements of a tired man trying hard not to wake the remaining members of his family. When someone showed up at your front door early on a Sunday morning, most people knew it was serious: if not, why would they disturb your sacred time?

Apprehensively, Ben opened the front door, while still tying the waist of his white robe together.

"It had better not be Claire's money that she left for Alannah."

The shock of the statement caught him off-guard, his eyes widened, pupils dilating rapidly as the fear became clearly visible on his face. He quickly tried to recover and conceal his emotions, badly faking a morning yawn in order to buy him the necessary time to think on the fly, a few extra seconds to get his mental faculties together but it was all too obvious, all too clear to see.

"I don't know what you're talking about Jack." He looked away from me, away from my glare. "And I don't know why you're here on a Sunday morning discussing money. Have you been drinking hard again? Hitting the vodka?"

It was a poor effort to deflect his guilt on me with the drinking jibe. I'd played this game before and with far better players than him.

"Ben," I stepped close to him, close enough for

him to feel my breath. "I've got a job from Chase Martin."

His face dropped. The game was up and he knew it.

"Alright, alright." He hushed me, stepped away from the front door, and closed the door behind him. "I'll listen to you, just don't wake the family."

"You'll do more than listen, you'll answer my questions unreservedly too. You hear me?"

He nodded, meekly.

Ben was slight, clean cut, late thirties. Brown hair, bushy eyebrows, and I was sure he'd have a hairy back, not that I ever wanted to check. A cop by day, a family man by night, and an idiot twenty-four hours a day, seven days a week.

He'd seen some of the worst the streets of Chicago had to offer, some gruesome crimes and some senseless killings, recently losing a partner in a gunfight with gangbangers. His once boyish looks were fading to middle-age, the bags under his eyes becoming more pronounced and the previously thin lines on his forehead now deep and furrowed. His waistline too was beginning to bulge and his overall health was on a steep downward trajectory: hypertension, stomach ulcers and high cholesterol were his new normal. But that didn't mean I was going to go easy on him, far from it.

When I first started dating his sister, he wasn't happy. He thought I was too tough, too rough, and

41

full of too much violent stuff to care about her. He barely spoke a word to me until the day of Claire's and my wedding, which we held in the beautiful town of Madison, Wisconsin, for just a handful of family and friends in an historic chapel, St. Patrick's, there he shook my hand, told a bad joke, and afterwards at the reception shared a beer. That was the start of an awkward relationship, at best. You know what they say: you can choose your friends but you can't choose your family, and certainly not your in-laws. But as the old joke goes: what's the difference between in-laws and outlaws?... outlaws are wanted. You're thrown into social situations with people who, were you not obligated, you almost certainly wouldn't bother seeing at all.

"What are you doing with Chase Martin?" Ben asked.

I didn't answer.

"Ok. Ok." He touched my elbow and led me down the path that went to their front gate, further from the family. "I lost money with Chase Martin. An investment gone wrong."

Again, I didn't respond.

"He's not a nice guy, Jack. He's the scum of the earth. A group of us invested with him, he ripped us all off, and has almost bankrupted me. Ruined everything I've worked hard to gain. I want nothing to do with him. I've tried to arrest him for fraud, but it's no use, he's always got these high-powered lawyers protecting his sorry ass. Everything he does is about money, and everything he does is fraudulent. He's a con."

He was starting to get flustered, but still no response from me. I let him stew.

Silence can be the heaviest of statements. Under the pressure of silence, under the thunderous weight of quiet, a nervous person can try to fill the gaps with information, try and fill the quiet with knowledge. Sometimes lies, but often the truth. And what usually happens is that a person spills so much more than they ever intended to. I'm sure he did it when the roles were reversed and he was a cop interrogating someone, but that didn't mean he wasn't just as susceptible to it as well.

Finally, he sighed.

"Ok, Jack. Yes, I invested Claire's money."

"That money was for Alannah's college fund. She left that behind in her will for Alannah." I grunted, turning to face him square on and look him in the eye. "That wasn't your money to invest."

I could feel my blood rising. I was angry. And getting more so. At what he'd done but also at the thought of anything associated with Claire. It seemed like a slap in her face, the undoing of her kind gesture through his own stupidity. But for now, I controlled my emotions. I had to, for the sake of the case, for my own sanity, and most of all for young Millie. She needed me to solve this case and get her back home safe, if I lost my temper now it could only hinder that from happening. I needed Ben to talk, to unburden himself with the truth for me to use every bit of information he provided to go after the guilty party.

"I know. I know. You don't think I feel horrible about this? This fight against Chase Martin has almost made us bankrupt, and the stress of it all has nearly sent me over the edge. I'm a man on the edge, Jack. I don't know how much more I can take. I've worked hard all my life for what I've got. And now it's all gone. And my health is going too. The cost of medical bills is almost too much for us to bear. And it's all Chase Martin's fault."

"My heart bleeds," I said bluntly. "And what do you mean 'worked hard'? That money was from Claire. You didn't do anything for it."

I know he was having a hard time of it, and I did genuinely care about his health issues and where he was going to find the money to pay for his medical treatment, but I was angry too and not in the mood to be emotionally blackmailed by his tale of woe.

He held up his hands in surrender. "I put my own money in too. Everything. Chase told us that the investment was foolproof. He told us that we would triple our money in a month. Just about guaranteed it to us. But…" He sighed and ran his hand over his hair. "But of course, it was too good to be true. The prick was setting us up. Took us for a ride. As soon as we invested the money, the company declared bankruptcy. We lost everything."

"Bad timing?"

"Not a chance. It was a house of cards just waiting to fall. After we lost the money, I did some digging and found out that he's run this scam before. Many times, as it happens. We weren't the first group of people to fall into his web of lies. The companies—"

"The companies?"

"Like I said, it's not the first time he's run this scam. He runs it about once a year. The companies are owned in untouchable places, such as the Cayman Islands, and there's no information on them. Even as a cop, I can't access who owns the companies or why they went bankrupt. In my investigations, I found out that Chase Martin is a horrible investor and an even worse human being."

"But a good scammer."

"Exactly. He's a great salesman. A con artist. An actor, really. The only way he makes money is by ripping people off. And this time, he ripped off ten former army soldiers, including me. Destroyed some lives in the process."

"And how did you get involved?"

"An ex-army brother in arms, Chuck Kowalski, who I've kept in touch with over the years, he's had some really low times, struggled with PTSD, but he was coming out of it, starting to see the light at the end of the tunnel. He thought this investment was going to put him on a new path. Even borrowed money from his elderly mother to make up the full amount. He was excited, he convinced me to meet with Chase, and boy, was Chase a smooth talker." He trailed off for a moment and I could see the anger simmering beneath the surface. "I met with him once and I was sold on the investment. It sounded perfect. Chase told us that he'd received an inside tip, and Chase was going to invest his own money as well."

The vulnerable make the best scam targets. When someone is down, when their defenses are weakened, they look for a way out, an exit from the current path they're on.

"Making ten ex-army men angry is a dangerous game to play."

"Well, he played it. And it seems he has enough money to get away with it. We're out of options and can't afford to do anything else anyway. We tried the legal route, initially, but he knows we can't afford to take it to court. He'll tie it up for years. We don't have the resources for a fight like that, and he knows it. We'll be bankrupt before we can get a decision in the courts. It's not fair." Ben closed his eyes, lowered his head to his hand and massaged his forehead. With a sigh, he raised his head and met my unyielding gaze. "I'm really sorry, Jack, I really am. I was only trying to do the best for my family, for my little girl. It's so hard these days, to afford a good education, a house, even bringing a baby into the world just costs so much money, I only wanted to make it so Alannah didn't have to worry about any of that. Now she'll be even worse off."

He shrugged as though accepting this fate.

"So what's your involvement with Chase? I hope you're not considering investing."

I scoffed at the thought.

"You know me, Ben. That's not my style." I stared at him, searching his face for clues. "I can't tell you what I'm working on, but I need you to tell me something—where were you on Saturday morning?"

"Yesterday." He flinched. Pulled on his ear lobe. "I was out fishing. Getting some time to myself."

With his small grooming movements, Ben was dispersing the nervous energy of his falsehood. To a casual observer, that small error might be overlooked as a normal gesture, it might be written off as the nerves of an unstable person under difficult circumstances, but I wasn't a casual observer, and this was not a casual conversation.

"Anyone able to verify that you were out fishing yesterday morning?"

"Sorry, Jack. I was alone. Not even a fish to verify it." He tried to convey a fake chuckle, only highlighting his lie.

I almost felt offended that he thought his amateur attempts at deception would work on an old pro like me. I stared at him for a long moment.

"If you hear anything about Chase or that money, you need to call me right away."

He nodded his response, and I left with the information, heading back to my waiting Chevy.

But I knew it wasn't the whole truth. I knew he was holding something back. And I also knew that I was going to find out what it was, no matter the consequences.

A girl's life was on the line and time was running out fast.

CHAPTER 6

THE MOST crucial stage of any private investigation work wasn't the inspection of the crime scene or scenario to be investigated, it wasn't the identifying of potential witnesses or suspects, or the interviewing of those individuals. Nope. The most essential step, the step that showed an investigator what he needed to know the most, was the collection of information gathered about the person hiring the investigator. The person who should be beyond reproach, but seldom is.

Ordinary, regular people with ordinary, regular lives don't hire private investigators. People who are in trouble, people who have messed up, hire investigators. And more often than not, they're holding something back. And what they are holding back was often of imminent importance.

By the time I had arrived back in my office after talking to my brother-in-law, Casey May already had a file on my desk. The beauty of investigating in the age of the internet was that the information was readily available at a few clicks of a mouse.

Chase Martin grew up in a poor family in Detroit,

his father was a blue collar worker, his mother a housewife. The youngest of three brothers and one sister, he was always striving for attention, always trying to gather a response.

His school records didn't show anything outstanding, nor did the reviews of his academic record at university. His yearbook quote was brief and unimaginative, 'I play to win', but it pretty much summed Chase up. I could see from his photo he was not a bad looking kid. I suppose that helps when you plan to spend your life charming people then ripping them off.

He had had one run-in with the law when he was fifteen for trying to sell fake handbags at a festival, but other than that, his nose was clean. On paper at least.

He'd spent ten years working for a small investment firm, before branching out on his own. And that's where his career really took a turn for the better, or worse, depending on your perspective. The claims of fraudulent behavior were long, and varied, but nothing stuck, nothing held up in a court of law.

He was either lucky, innocent, or very cunning.

I was going with the third option.

"Anything from Ben?" Casey asked.

"A hint, but nothing more. I don't buy his alibi, but I didn't see any evidence of a kidnapping." I sat behind the desk in my office, flicking through the file on Chase Martin.

To the untrained eye my office was a dump, my desk had a virtual pyramid of old random case notes piled up in the middle, intermingled with old newspapers, random automobile and pick-up truck magazines, empty packs of cigarettes, even a couple of empty pizza boxes; OK, perhaps more than just a couple of boxes, but this wasn't an interior design project, it was my workplace. It sure wasn't pretty or organized, but then as Einstein once said, 'If a cluttered desk is a sign of a cluttered mind, of what then, is an empty desk a sign?' I liked it that way and it worked for me.

"What've you got?" I asked Casey.

"I'm still working on the list of his most recent investors, but I think you're going to enjoy your first interview this morning. The location anyway. The ex-wife, Tanya, works as a bartender not far from here in Logan Square. She usually works the dead shift— Sunday morning from eleven."

"Perfect." I smiled.

The 11am shift in a bar usually meant few customers, and small tips from those who did arrive, but that was good for me. A few dollars thrown in the right direction after the first drink and she'd be all ears, and hopefully a bit of mouth too, I needed some information and hoped I could get her to talk.

I looked at my watch. Enough time to down a coffee or two—double strength and black—while I read the full file on Chase Martin, and then find myself at the bar by 11am.

"Keep me updated on what you find out about the surveillance footage of the area." I nodded to Casey as I walked back out the door. "I'm going to check out the ex-wife. See if she can give us a hint."

Within the hour, I was three coffees in, well-read on Chase's life, and ready to walk through the doors of the Malt and Hops bar in Logan Square.

"What'll it be, hon?" asked an attractive but world worn looking blond in a low-cut top.

I liked the name 'hon.' It's instantly welcoming, warming, and transported me back to a time when my grandmother used to bake cookies on Sunday morning. My Grandmother and I were close. I'll never forget the words she wanted on her headstone: "What are you doing in here with that hammer?" She liked that sort of humor. But I wasn't there for jokes, I was there to talk with Chase Martin's ex-wife, and Millie's mother, Tanya.

"I've had a rough month. Just after a beer and an ear." I threw a fifty on the table, and Tanya's eyes lit up. "Keep the drinks flowing and the conversation rolling."

She poured a pint of beer, with a head slightly too big, and placed it on the bar in front of me.

The bar was too bright for my liking, too many windows. Its menu was too long, with far too many fancy options, and the smell was pine fresh. Someone had recently mopped the floor, the long wooden bar was wiped clean, and the area outside the door even had green plants.

Not my sort of place, but it must've worked for some.

"So what's up?"

"My Dad's been diagnosed with cancer." It was a lie, an attempt to strike a chord with Tanya, my father was long gone, and I was pleased about that too, the sorry SOB that he was, always beating on my mother, until I came of age that is and turned the tables on him. "He doesn't have long left. It's been a rough ride."

"Oh, sweetheart." She reached out and touched my hand. 'Sweetheart' was a name I liked as well. "I know how that feels. My father has only a few months left. Cancer as well. It's a terrible thing to go through."

"Oh, I'm sorry," I said. "I don't want to upset you too."

"It's okay, it's good to talk," she said. "You can't bottle this type of thing up inside or it'll explode. It's better to talk about it and let all these things out."

"I don't have anyone to talk to about this. No one close enough. Not since…" I trailed off with a little shake of the head. "At least I've got the kids. They're too young to really understand but they're a good distraction, really keep me busy. How about you?"

She smiled, and I could tell she was picturing Millie. "I have one girl with my ex-husband. Luckily, my father has enough energy to still play with her. Millie, she's only five, but hopefully she'll remember the time she got to spend with her grandfather."

"They're good together?"

"The best. My father could play with Millie for days and never get bored. I think, now that his time is coming, he realizes how he should've spent more time at home when I was young, and looks at Millie as a way to make up for it." Her smile was broad. "And their personalities are just the same. They're both as strong-willed and as cheeky as each other."

I spent the next five minutes spinning a long lie about kids and history, and I felt bad about doing it. There was something calming about Tanya, a gentle soul with a caring touch, that I found comforting, even alluring. But I wasn't there to judge people, I wasn't there to make friends—I was there to try and find a little girl. Her little girl, Millie. Knowing what I knew about Millie's kidnapping, which Tanya wasn't even aware of, felt like the worst kind of deception. But I told myself it was the only way, the only way I stood a chance of finding her. I had to let it play out. And so, despite the temptation, I said nothing, I couldn't, and wouldn't, not at this stage anyway, but that's not to say if things changed for the worse in the next few days or even hours that I wouldn't. After all, a mother had a right to know and Chase Martin be dammed. But right now, even she was a suspect.

"My father has been talking about euthanasia," she

poured me another beer. "He doesn't want his granddaughter to remember him at his worst. He doesn't want Millie to see him as weak and frail. And he's so sold on legacy. He needs to leave something behind for Millie. He always worked hard, so hard, and he was always honorable, but he had nothing. He's got no money to leave behind, he's got no savings, and he's got nothing to leave her. That must be hard to work through. To know that you've left nothing behind."

"Are you doing it all alone then? Bringing up Millie by yourself?"

"Well, that's another story." She shook her head, and poured herself a glass of soda. "My ex and I signed a pre-nup. I thought I was marrying for love and family, so the pre-nup didn't matter. My father was angry about that, and when the marriage fell apart after a year and a half, he was really angry. Especially when it comes to child support. My ex just has no idea how much it really costs to feed, clothe, house and generally look after a child. And besides, I'm too ashamed to ask for more. Dad stayed in touch with Chase, that's my ex, thought he might be able to coax him around to giving more. Until recently Chase kept him at arms' length. But," She held back a nice smile. "After my father was diagnosed with cancer, Chase was more open to contact and letting him help out with childcare, things like that, whenever it's needed. Chase understands that Dad doesn't have long left, so is helping out. I never knew my ex had a heart, so that was nice."

"Pre-nup, eh?" I grunted. "That's pretty crazy. I've never met anyone who's signed one of those before."

And then, for just one moment, I saw a glint of anger in her eyes, a fleeting moment of disguised rage. "Don't get me started."

The door to the bar opened behind us, and an elderly well-dressed couple walked in.

I nodded to Tanya, knocked back the rest of my beer, and left her to the couple.

There was anger behind Tanya's wall.

Perhaps enough anger to take revenge on the man she hated.

CHAPTER 7

RUBY JONES wasn't hard to track.

She posted about her every movement on social media, her every step was a walking documentation of her vapid boring life. She was pretty, I guess, in a younger girl sort-of-way, tall with long red hair and the voice of a playboy bunny. Too high-pitched and squeaky for my liking. She was all a bit ice cream and sprinkles for me, all looks and no substance, an empty vessel that made the most noise, which tended to be a whine that was mainly about herself.

After I talked with Tanya, I followed Ruby's steps and found her taking selfies outside The Bean—one of Chicago's many famous sculptures. Shaped like a giant bean, around fifteen-feet high, and made of reflective metal, it was a piece of art that I could appreciate. It was a conversation point, something to marvel at, something to take photos of. But the central feature of Ruby's photos was always the same: herself. This pose, that pose, a sideways glance at the camera, then one from the other side, eyes front, a smile, a frown, a bit of cleavage, some leg. To say the girl was self-obsessed would be a gross understatement.

If she could have married herself, I'm sure she would have done it.

She silently screamed 'Me! Me! Me!' all day long, constantly checking herself out in the windows of shops and cars, and boy did she like what she saw. It was funny, as although I could understand her physical appeal to some, to me she was ugly. An effortless grace, an intellect, and sharp wit was attractive to me, and she had none of the above. In fact, she had a downright deficit in those departments.

At mid-afternoon on a Sunday, the area around the Bean was filled with tourists and families. There were couples with strollers, the middle aged with their adult children, large extended families with grandparents, aunties, uncles and cousins in tow, and lots and lots of sightseeing tourists. Sitting on the park bench, staring back at the city behind the Bean, it made me think about kids. As I entered my forties, the notion that I might have kids was becoming less of a possibility, still a chance, but less so. Did I even want kids? With Claire, absolutely. But the thought of letting the past go, leaving my deceased wife behind, was still heartbreaking.

She was killed in a school shooting, a teacher caught in the line of fire, trying to protect one of her students. It broke my heart every morning when I woke and reached across to her cold empty side of the bed. No one had been there since, nor did I expect or plan there to be.

The man who provided the shooter with the weapon, Hugh Guthrie, was due to be in court the next day, facing charges of murdering a fellow newscaster. I had a hand in that arrest, finally giving myself a sense of justice for Claire. Guthrie had set the school shooter up, pushed the shooter to the limits, and then armed him with the tools to make it happen, all for the purpose of making a documentary.

I could've sent Hugh Guthrie to the afterlife, but I decided to let the courts deal with the scum.

Claire wanted kids. She loved them and wanted to have two. A boy and a girl was her dream. I went along with it, I went along with most things she wanted, but never really gave it much thought. Now, with Millie, those thoughts were running through my head, running wild and tormenting me.

Deep down, I think the answer was yes, I did want kids. Or at least I would have liked to have had them with my Claire. But did I want them with someone else one day? I wasn't so sure. Undecided, I guess. But if I did then that would mean moving on from Claire, and I wasn't sure I was ready for that, if I ever would be. To do so would feel like a betrayal of her.

Ruby Jones was still striking poses in her low-cut yellow dress. She looked like an emaciated model to me, with long skinny legs that seemed to run on forever. Although most of her life was tracked via social media, there was a patch of radio silence yesterday, the day of the kidnapping, the first time she hadn't posted on social media for a day in more than a year. It was a big red flag right there. Although correlation doesn't automatically mean causation, it was extremely suspicious, that's for sure.

I took a deep breath, patted down my hair, and made my way over to her.

"Do you know where the nearest Starbucks is?" I questioned when in range.

"Starbucks?" She looked annoyed that I interrupted her selfies, that I had dared enter the sacred space of one so great and that she was far superior to me. She pointed down the road dismissively. "That way," she said with a condescending flick of the back of her hand.

Before she could turn away, I followed up.

"One of my followers said that the Starbucks near the Bean was the best Starbucks in the country." I tapped the metal structure with my right hand. "I hope it is, because I need a coffee right now."

Ruby looked me up and down, clearly doubting I even knew what 'followers' were, let alone whether I actually had any.

"Followers?" she said with a marked air of disdain.

"Yeah. On Instagram. I've got over 500,000 followers, and whenever I travel, the locals are more than happy to give me advice. Normally pretty good advice too."

"You have 500,000 followers on Instagram?" She was shocked, and rightfully so. I didn't even know how to navigate Instagram, let alone post on it. "I don't believe you, old man. Why would anyone want to follow you?"

I had to give her credit, she was forthright and to the point. And I won't lie, the 'old man' dig hurt.

I was feeling it more and more of late, picking up constant niggling injuries at the gym, most recently a sprained ankle, but I wasn't going to let her know that.

"Ok." I shrugged. "You don't have to believe me. Thanks for the directions. Have a nice day."

I began to walk away and that confidence caught her attention. Most men would have been intimidated by her looks but not me. And it clearly threw her.

"Wait. Do you really have that many followers?"

"I do."

"What's your handle?"

If an 'old man' said that he had that many followers, then I'll admit, even my curiosity would be peaked. Luckily for me, the system could be manipulated easily and Casey knew how to do that. Followers could be bought, pictures backdated, and profiles set up within a few minutes.

While I was talking to Tanya, Casey set up a fake profile with my smiling mug on the front, and a range of pictures throughout LA, my face nicely Photoshopped into pictures with celebrities. The page would only be available for a day to convince Ruby of my celeb status, and then deleted.

"I'm a movie producer. I'm traveling from LA, looking for new talent for my next movie, and I think that she's right here in Chicago. There's something about the warmth to the women in this city. Maybe it's all the cold weather?" I stepped closer to her. "My Instagram handle is @Movies.Producer.LA."

Sometimes the simplest profile can be the most convincing. Ruby scanned the profile quickly, saw the pictures of me on movie sets, at award ceremonies with the great and the good, even on a yacht with a certain former president, and was convinced. I'm sure if she spent more than five seconds looking at any one of those pictures, she would see that they were fake, but I wasn't going to give her that chance.

"You should join me for that coffee," I stated confidently. It wasn't a question, more an assertion, and she did as instructed.

She smiled, and for the first time since I'd been watching her, she put her phone away and followed my lead.

The walk to the coffee shop was filled with small talk, I was doing my best to name drop, casually of course, and Ruby was doing her best to look fabulous. She wanted in on that movie. She explained that she had 50,000 followers, she was famous, and she was ready to hit the big time. She talked of the acting classes she'd taken, the modelling she'd done, how she could sing and that she had even once worked as a dancer. It was all too obvious what she was after. I pretended to be interested, as if impressed with such a boring list of credentials.

"What's your account handle?" I asked.

"A.Star.Is.Born.Chicago."

I took out my phone and looked at her profile.

"How come you took a day off yesterday, you've posted consistently until then, some good material, but it's unwise to kick back and take a break," I said pretending to be surprised at the absence of any postings for the day in question.

Her one-word answer was sudden – 'sick.' Too quick, and too rehearsed.

We entered Starbucks and ordered our coffees.

"Got anything to tie you to Chicago?" I asked after we sat down on the outdoor seats along Michigan Ave. "Boyfriend? Husband? Kids?"

"No kids. And I don't want any in the future, either," she answered. "But my family is here. My father, Frank Jones, would do anything for me and its kind of nice to have that support. I could ask him to drive to New York City and buy a salmon bagel for me, and he'd do it without question."

"Sounds like a great dad."

"Not really. Before he got sober five years ago, he was violent, and he used to beat my mother and I when he got drunk. Now that he's sober, he'd do anything for us. He's a mechanic, but he's got mob connections, and he loves us. He's still the centerpiece of my family."

"Boyfriend?"

"My dad? No. He's still married to my mother."

"I meant you," I smiled. It was clear that Ruby was about as sharp as a bowling ball.

"I do have a boyfriend, and he'd be happy to move anywhere. He's rich. We've got a good life, but I think it's time for the next adventure."

"Does he have kids?"

"Not really."

"Not really?" I laughed. "What does that mean?"

"I mean," she paused for a few moments and bit her lip. "He does, but she just gets in the way. She'll be gone soon anyway."

"Gone? Why?" I leaned forward.

The question caught Ruby off-guard and she sat up straight. "Her mother wants more time with the kid. That'll be good for Chase and me anyway. We can travel more then. Maybe even move to LA. It's somewhere I've always wanted to work."

My list of suspects was growing, and that wasn't helping me one bit.

CHAPTER 8

SOMETIMES THE smallest action could annoy me. Like the way those born into money and privilege hold their little finger out when they drink. That annoyed me.

But at least those who were born rich didn't know any better. What annoyed me even more was when people faked it to look like they were born with a silver spoon in their mouth, like they were from good stock or something, and were better than the rest of us mere grunts. And that was especially so when it was someone I already found annoying. Like Chase Martin doing it, while delicately sipping his tiny little espresso from one of those silly miniature cups. Yeah, that'll do it, gets my blood boiling every time.

And yes, most things I had discovered about Chase Martin so far had annoyed me. I had no doubt that Ben was telling the truth when he said that Chase was running scams. Everything about him shouted con artist, at least to me; I guess to those he managed to con he came off as confident and sophisticated, a man who knew what he was talking about and who would look after them and especially look after their precious money, those who didn't know any better.

His apartment wasn't built for children—there were prized and delicate artifacts everywhere, almost waiting to be broken by an over enthusiastic child, which spoke volumes about his authoritarian and regimented parenting style, where he no doubt stamped out any exuberant free play in favor of organized and controlled order. I was sure some of the artifacts were bought off the black market and that their legality was questionable at best. It wouldn't surprise me if they were smuggled into the US in breach of the laws of this great country, as well as the laws of wherever in the world they first originated.

I was surprised he even bothered with Millie at all. She didn't seem to fit his lifestyle.

"Tell me about Ruby." I sat down on the couch.

"Ruby? You think she's involved?" Chase finished his espresso and ran his hand through his hair, flicking it back at the last minute with a flamboyant confidence that annoyed me even more.

He walked over to a grandiose armchair opposite, practically a throne, a chair worthy of Hugh Hefner, and sat down. "I don't know."

"Does she get along with Millie?"

"Well, no. I think she finds her an inconvenience. To be fair, Millie doesn't get along with her either." He shook his head thoughtfully. "Millie is a lot like her mother—feisty and with an angry streak. That didn't sit well with Ruby. I've been seeing Ruby for around six months, and the first couple of months I tried to bring Ruby and Millie together, but it didn't work. For whatever reason, they never ended up getting along."

I ignored the obvious that Chase himself was the problem and reason for this.

"Do you think Ruby is capable of hurting Millie?"

"I wouldn't have thought so, but I suppose the truth is I don't know. She isn't the deepest soul I've ever met, or the most intelligent." He shook his head again and looked away. "Over the past month, she wouldn't even come to the apartment when Millie was here. She wanted me to give full custody of Millie to Tanya. Asked me to do it several times, in fact. She wanted me to sign away all my rights and never see Millie again."

"When did she first ask you to do that?"

"Last month." A realization sunk into his head, and he stood, pacing back and forth. "She couldn't, could she?" He pondered the thought for a moment, like he was pitching the scenario, weighing it in his head. "No, I don't think she could, but she could've hired someone." His hand tightened into a fist. "She didn't want Millie around. She wanted to move to LA, and for me to fund her little Instagram life."

"She doesn't have her own money?"

"Not a cent to her name. Her father is a mechanic and her mother is a retired nurse. A real low-class life and background." He raised his finger in the air. That annoyed me as well. "Maybe, that's why she needs the money? Yeah, that's why she needs the million dollars. To fund her move to LA. She needs me to pay her the money and then take off to LA without me. She wants to take my money and run."

"That's a possibility."

"She wants to continue to live the lavish life without me. I should've seen it. I should've seen that she was going to use me. It was always going to happen. Well, she's messed with the wrong person this time. She will curse the day she ever crossed me, ever crossed Chase Martin."

He said the last bit with an arrogant emphasis, like he was underlining his own name and really wanted to add 'the great' in front of it too. He certainly had a high opinion of himself and his own stock value but all I saw in front of me was a loser of the highest order, despite how many zeros there were after the balance of his bank account. The measure of a man was not, and never would be, how much money he had.

His face was registering anger now, which had its uses, but for now, I needed him to be rational so I decided to try to calm things down.

"We don't know it's her yet. She's a suspect at the moment, that's all. Is there anywhere she would've kept Millie, while she goes about her daily business?"

"'Business?' Hah!" he scoffed. "Posting those stupid photos all day isn't a business!" He continued to pace the floor. "But no, not really. She still lives with her Mom and Dad, near their mechanic shop. Dirty place. Her mother and father wouldn't stand for it. They hate me, but they seemed to be good people."

The intercom buzzed.

We stared at each other.

Chase looked at his phone, opening an app that gave him streaming footage of the front door. "It's Damon. Millie's Grandfather." He looked worried. "What am I going to tell him?"

I shrugged. "Can you just ignore it, pretend you're not home?"

"Oh." He leaned his head back in realization. "He was supposed to pick up Millie today for a few hours. I forgot."

The intercom buzzed again.

"Tell him that Millie is at a play date with a friend and you've forgotten to tell him."

"That's it." Chase clicked his fingers and pointed his index finger at me triumphantly. "Of course. Good thinking, Jack."

He buzzed Damon into the building, and within a few minutes, he was at the apartment door.

"Damon." Chase greeted him with a solid handshake. "Come on in. So sorry but I forgot you were coming today. Millie is at a playdate at a friend's place. I should have let you know but it completely slipped my mind, what with the deluge of work I have going on at the moment: lots of new clients, lots of new opportunities, you know the sort of thing."

Damon raised his eyebrows slightly. He was clearly ex-army. A spotless polo shirt tucked into his ironed jeans, white sneakers that were cleaned recently, perhaps even daily.

He was immediately suspicious of my presence.

"This is Jack. A friend of mine." Chase introduced us.

We shook hands. His grip was strong.

"Pleased to meet you, Damon."

"Friend?" He raised his eyebrows again. "You're not the usual type of friend that Chase has. Usually, his friends are blonde, twenty-years old, and have had a lot of cosmetic surgery."

"That's me," I said with a wry smile. "Except the blonde bit, obviously."

He laughed. The tension was broken.

"Army?" I asked.

"For a while. Ten years. Then I left and became a mechanic. Not a lavish life like this." He opened his hands wide to indicate his disdain for Chase's opulent life. "You risk your life for your country and you never get paid like this. But you wouldn't understand that, would you, Chase? What was it that you said to me once? That it's not about working harder, it's about working smarter. I guess the rest of us just aren't as smart as you, hey Chase?"

"Life isn't fair," Chase added. "And it's very unbecoming of you to blame me for my obvious success. I've worked hard for what I've achieved, and I won't apologize for it, to you or anyone, Damon."

The tension was back. Thick in the room like a dirty fog that lingered heavy and oppressive.

We stood there for a few moments, three men who wouldn't take a backward step, until finally Chase moved things forward.

"I'm sorry, Damon. I forgot you were coming today." Chase put his hands in the pockets of his chinos. "How about you come around next week and play with Millie?"

"I'm disappointed she isn't here. She's all I've got to look forward to at the moment," Damon responded and turned to me. "I haven't got long left, you see. I'm ill. The doctors reckon I've got six months, but I'll be gone before then." He looked back towards Chase. "So a missed playdate with my only granddaughter is a big deal for me. After all, how many do I have left in such a short period, before neither of us can see each other again. I know we don't always see eye to eye, but next time I'd ask you to respect that fact, and make sure this doesn't happen again, for her sake more than mine."

Chase sort of grunted a non-committal response.

"I'm sorry to hear about your illness," I said to Damon.

"It's alright. My wife went a few years ago, and apart from Millie, I haven't got that much else left here. I'm looking forward to seeing my wife again."

I admired his faith. I didn't quite know where I stood on that front. I wanted to believe, who wouldn't in my shoes, but I didn't want to delude myself either.

"Look, sorry to be blunt," Chase interrupted. He wasn't sorry. "But Jack is here on business, so I'll give you a call when Millie's available."

"Thanks." Damon nodded to Chase. "Nice to meet you, Jack."

He shook my hand again, it felt like he was almost sizing me up.

Chase shut the door behind Damon, waited a few moments, and then turned back to me.

"What's next? Should I be putting pressure on Ruby?"

"Not yet. If it's her, we don't want her to hurt Millie." I walked towards the door. "Casey and I are going to investigate further, so right now, sit tight and get the money ready. I don't want it to come to that, but time's running out so it might. And I need you to be ready for that possibility."

CHAPTER 9

INVESTIGATING HAD changed a lot over my career.

When I started twenty-five years ago, the internet was something that nerds talked about, downloading their pixelated images at a painfully slow speed. Facebook wasn't around to catch up with friends, Wikipedia didn't exist for general research, there was no Amazon or Goodreads to leave witty and punchy five-star reviews of your favorite book, and young boys had to go to their father's adult magazine stash for a look at a naked woman.

The internet had changed everything about our lives, making the world so much smaller. Paradoxically simpler but also more complex at the same time. Sometimes I harped on about the easier days before it's development, but it had its purposes.

I found out more about Hugh Guthrie's first court appearance in twenty minutes than I could've in a whole day investigating in the years gone past.

The result sent me into a tailspin of shock.

The man who provided the gun to my wife's killer, the man who I held responsible for her murder, had made an appearance before the court, and had his murder charge thrown out.

With the aid of the internet, I researched what happened. The clearance on one of his search warrants wasn't authorized by the right person, and the evidence had to be thrown out. There was one administrative error after another, almost like they wanted him to get off. Officially, the case was thrown out because five main pieces of the evidence couldn't be used, but it was all linked back to the incorrectly filed paperwork. Part of me wondered if Guthrie himself had a hand in achieving that outcome. A few dollars there, and a few dollars here, and who knows what could've been achieved? Guthrie was certainly cunning enough to try it.

Before the murder of newscaster Brian Gates, Guthrie had manufactured a documentary about school shootings, in an effort to arm the teachers, and had pushed a young man to his breaking point. The teenager used a gun provided by Guthrie to shoot up the school, and in the process, murdered my wife.

Despite the fact that he admitted to me that he set the whole thing up for the purpose of a documentary, the police couldn't pin that on him. I had his recorded confession, however it was thrown out of court because it was obtained under potential coercion.

I had no other evidence, however I rested on the fact that he would at least go down for the other murder.

Now that was out the window as well.

The rage that built inside me threatened to explode, but I kept it at bay with deep breathing exercises.

This was no time to lose control. There would be plenty of time for that later.

Now, I had to focus on saving a little girl.

It was true what Ben had told me—Chase Martin's list of fraudulent activities was as long as my arm. Nothing stuck, of course, but the accusations were available on the internet, where disgruntled investor after disgruntled investor lined up to give account of his activities. Rather tellingly, many of his accusers voiced concerns of censorship, with stories of other websites having been closed down after serious legal threats from Chase's lawyers. The ones that remained were new postings, only a couple of months old and in all likelihood, they would be deleted before long too, keeping cyberspace clean of accusation so he could strike again and some poor unsuspecting victim.

A bit more digging and I was starting to get a profile of Chase Martin that suggested he was a scammer from way back. Despite a fairly unimpressive grade point average, he had managed to land a place at a pretty good college, all thanks to a reference from some wealthy lady he did gardening for on the weekends as a teenager, and it seemed she had paid his tuition fees as part of the bargain. She was a former academic and a patron of the college, no doubt he charmed her into thinking of him as the son she never had. That, or he was providing some other services for a lonely divorcee which she paid for with something other than cold hard cash.

While at college, he managed to buddy up to rich kids with connections so that, despite barely passing, he managed to land a very sought after position as soon as he graduated, with the family investment firm of one of his supposed friends. After 10 years, he started his own firm and managed to con a bunch of clients into following him. His former employers tried to sue for breach of contract, but he had it well planned and they couldn't quite pin it on him.

Poor investment choices led to most clients returning to their former firm within the year, but that didn't matter, because now he had his formula: scam his investors, get his payout, move on.

His love life followed a similar pattern. Chase Martin certainly was shaping up to be a nasty piece of work.

From what I could see, it seemed that he'd run the yearly scam for five years—setting up a new company in another country, convincing suckers to invest, and then declaring the business bust.

"I've just found something." Casey stormed into my office, frantic, waving her phone in the air.

"The new iPhone?"

"Ha ha, very funny. I'm gonna need a pay rise for

that." She grinned. "Any chance?"

I laughed.

"Oh well, maybe you'll change your mind after you see this. I've turned up something on the case." She smiled. "A photo."

She turned to my computer, tapped a few keys and brought up the internet on the screen.

"How did you know my password?" I asked.

"Are you serious?" she asked. "It's 'Claire123'. You're like an open book, Jack."

"A good book, I hope? A five-star book?"

"Something like that," she said with a smile.

"The computer said I needed a password at least eight characters long," I said. "So I tried 'Snow.White.and.the.Seven.Dwarfs,' but it was already taken."

"That's a terrible joke. And you didn't deliver it well either, Jack. Not that you ever do." Casey shook her head. "However, I did hear an expert on the news this morning say that in five years computers will have completely replaced paper. Well, I thought, that guy has never tried to wipe his butt with a laptop."

"Ha ha! Your joke was so much better than mine."

"They always are, Jack, but don't give up. There's hope for you yet."

Casey logged into her Facebook account and clicked on a link.

"I spent the morning looking at all the photos that were tagged with this location, or any location around the area, and painstakingly studied each photo. There were over a hundred photos tagged near the playground, and I studied each of them. Most of the photos were of kids on the swings, kids climbing trees, kids running around chasing a ball."

"Sounds creepy."

"If I was an old man that lived alone and I was studying pictures of children in playgrounds, then yes, it might've been creepy." She tapped a few more keys. "Look at this photo."

"I don't see anything."

"The picture is of a girl about to come down the slide, but look closer, over her right shoulder." Casey tapped the keyboard again, and zoomed in on the background.

"It's a van parked near the playground."

"And standing outside of that van is a little girl, and she matches Millie's description. Blonde hair, white coat, looks around five years old."

I sat forward. Casey was right. We had a lead.

The picture was blurry, the face of the girl wasn't clear, but it had to be Millie. She was outside the playground gates, looking at the back of the van, of which the door was slightly ajar. I stared at the photo, but couldn't make out what she was looking at.

"Any other photos?"

"Not that I could find. I even contacted the profile of the person who posted this, but they only took one photo that day."

"Who does the van belong to?"

"The van has a faded sign on the door for an old mechanic shop called 'The Top-Notch Service Garage.' I searched the internet for it, but found nothing. Then I called around the old-fashioned way, and found that the garage went out of business five years ago, and they operated out of two places. A gas station in Lincoln Park that has since been bought out by a large corporation, and a small warehouse in North Chicago, around an industrial area."

"And who bought the new warehouse?"

"It was never sold."

I thought for a moment, then reached for my book of contacts.

I picked up the phone, dialed the number of an old contact who lived in North Chicago. Jason Chapman was a former cop who owed me a lot of favors, and his knowledge of the area, and the people who lived in it, was second to none.

"Hasn't been activity in that area for years. It's dead over there. All the warehouses closed after some sort of safety scare, chemical spill or something, can't remember the exact details, but I think the new owners couldn't afford to clean it up," Chapman spoke quickly. "Probably five years since that place was used, and there must be five or six warehouses there. You could hide anything in that area."

"Trouble?" I asked.

"Only if you go looking for it," Chapman replied.

"And Jack, knowing you, you're going to go looking for it."

CHAPTER 10

BARELY EVEN a sound cut through the area, which we arrived at in the fading light of dusk.

It was the sort of place I half expected a tumbleweed to roll through. But even the wind refused to stir and there was nothing natural here either. Nature had turned her back on the area with even the birds seemingly staying away, as if the very air itself around the place was defiled and toxic. Sometimes places have a real, yet difficult to define, atmosphere, an eerie presence that transcends logic but strikes nonetheless at something deep and primal inside of us. So it was today, at the disused warehouse complex, which had a strange, almost unhealthy and invasive feel about it, like you might pick up a serious infection from a casual visit.

There were five warehouses in total, all with decrepit and faded signs hanging over the shed doors, and all with graffiti sprayed over the walls. From the brief research Casey conducted while we drove to the complex, she confirmed that the lot had been abandoned after a minor chemical spill five years ago. It made sense given the atmosphere of the place, but

81

apparently the area had been given the all-clear by the authorities; and on numerous occasions. But then money talks and who knows what the real story was. Whatever the truth of it was, the shoppers had simply stayed away no matter the official pronouncements of safety, with nobody wanting to go to shops that had a history of contamination. And so the warehouses subsequently closed down a little over a year later. The cost of redeveloping the area, and the rebranding, was too expensive. Instead, the area languished as an ode to a time long past.

The first warehouse was a former speedboat sales shop, the second and third warehouses were for competing truck repair dealerships, the fourth was an old diving shop, and the fifth, resting at the very back of the lot, furthest from the road and partially out of sight, was a former specialized mechanic shop. 'Top-Notch Service Garage' specialized in servicing the sort of cars that could be heard before seen, the sort that were driven by angry young men keen to make an impression on vulnerable young girls.

My Glock rested in its holster above my hip, concealed under my leather jacket. It was, however, unclipped and ready to go. My right hand rested on the weapon, ready to spring into action should the situation require it. And I had a feeling it would.

The tall chain link fence into the lot was open, barely hanging onto the frame, sagging badly in the middle. It squeaked as we tried to walk in, loud enough to cast an unwelcome warning echo through the lot. There were tire tracks through the puddles at the entrance, fresh tracks entering into the lot and heading towards the last warehouse at the back. They didn't reach the whole way there, fading out as they dried on the concrete but their overall direction was clear to see. This was interesting and concerning at the same time. We were not alone. Someone was in residence. On site in the here and now. And this was not the sort of place you came to without a nefarious reason.

We walked near the old warehouses, hugging them closely for protection and to remain concealed as we edged our way forward in the only eerie light, shining from the streetlight on the road behind us. Casey flanked my back, staying close, her hand on her weapon as well, and we slowly crept towards the warehouse at the end of the drive.

As we got closer, we could see a light. A flicker of electricity, clearly shining in the darkness, visible as a thin thread beneath the heavy garage doors.

Holding my hand back, I stopped Casey.

"There's someone there," I whispered. "It looks like the glow of a television. The power has been switched off to the site, so they must be using a generator to run it."

"Could be a homeless guy."

"With a generator? I don't think so." I looked around the lot. "Someone is hiding in there. Question is: why?"

"Maybe it's a bunch of squatters? Maybe a group of people who've stumbled across an old piece of equipment and are using it." Casey looked around. "That sort of thing happens sometimes."

"Could be," I said doubtfully, "but I don't think so." I checked the clip on my holster and my hand tightened around the familiar shape. "It's time for us to find out."

I signaled for Casey to move forward, and she jogged lightly over to the other side of the walkway.

We heard a noise.

A clear metal sound.

I drew my gun. Casey did the same. We were on high alert, ready to respond but not panicked.

The warehouse ahead of us had a large two-vehicle garage door, a small window next to the door, and a small door next to that. The flicker of light was soft, but it was enough to notice amongst the darkness. The sign for the 'Top-Notch Service Garage' hung low, faded in the years of inactivity. The driveway into the warehouse had crumbled, clumps of diseased looking weeds growing at random intervals along the path.

We heard another sound.

It was a person. Movement. Something happening. Someone moving.

The garage door moved upwards. The noise was loud, rusty metal scraping, echoing through the still night. It was dark inside. I couldn't see in.

My shoulder was against the wall of the adjoining warehouse, leaning in close to the shadows. Even from where I stood, I could barely see Casey on the other side of the street.

The darkness was heavy, covering our positions well, but the person could've spotted us already. Or heard us when we entered thanks to the scraping of the entrance fence. Movement was unusual here, and they wouldn't be expecting any wildlife around. Perhaps a rat, but they were right to be wary. It was not the sort of place you'd choose to frequent unless absolutely necessary.

I leaned forward to look into the area behind the garage door, but I couldn't make out the figure. I could see faint movement, but nothing more.

Again, there was a loud noise.

I spotted Casey. She was positioned well and waiting for my signal.

With our guns drawn, we inched forward into the night, every footstep heavy with the consequences of what we might find or encounter, and of what we might have to do. We were prepared for the worst and if necessary, for a fight. Both of us following the advice of gunslinger Wyatt Earp when he said, 'Take your time in a hurry': going into action with the greatest speed, but mentally unflustered by an urge to hurry.

As I moved to the next shadow against the wall, I

had a clearer view of the inside of the warehouse. I could see the outline of what was inside. There were two vehicles.

I stepped closer to take a better look.

There was a car.

And a van.

The car was dark in color and the van light, their exact hue difficult to discern with any certainty in the minimal light.

Could this be the white van we were looking for? Casey nodded towards the van with her eyebrows raised. She was clearly asking the same question.

We heard a muffled noise. Different this time. Not mechanical or metal but human. It could've been the noise of a child. Someone with a hand over their mouth being ushered along or moved against their will.

Then we heard the noise of a car door closing.

An engine roared into action, bringing the area to life. The second the headlights beamed in our faces, we couldn't see anything else. Against the darkness, it blinded us. I quickly moved against the wall, practically pushing myself into the brickwork to get out of the light. Casey leaned down.

A car roared between us, but I could see nothing else.

Casey jumped up and raced after the car, but there was no chance of catching it.

I considered opening a round from my gun, but I

didn't know who was in the car, where Millie was seated, or if she was even there.

The risk was too great.

I held back, finger on the trigger, gun pointed at the ground, watching the car turn into the distance. It screeched down the road, never slowing for the potholes, crashing through the half-open gate. The driver of the car wasn't going for a casual drive—they were escaping. They were running. And away from us. We were close, but not close enough. What did it all mean?

Casey ran back to stand next to me, gun still drawn, panting. Her eyes were fixated on the warehouse behind us.

"Did you get a look at who was driving? I didn't see anything."

"I saw nothing. The car was going too fast. And the headlights destroyed my night vision in a second." I turned back to the warehouse where the car had come from. "But we might get something from in there."

CHAPTER 11

THERE ARE certain places that I found it easier to think—driving in my Chevy with my favorite tunes, after a few beers on my couch, or at the dog park with my favorite mutt, Winston.

I was never supposed to like Winston, an always smiling golden retriever. He was my wife's idea, my wife's second love after me, or maybe even before me, who knows, but after her passing, he's become a part of my life.

I didn't want a dog, especially one that reminded me of my deceased wife, but my friends didn't want him, Claire's family said 'no,' and the pound was overfilled. Besides, the more I tried to get rid of him, the more I realized I needed to keep him, not just to provide him with a home but to help me deal with my grief. Sometimes it overwhelmed me, but whenever it did, Winston was always there with his unconditional happiness and enthusiasm, which would pull me through.

Watching him run free, so happy and wonderful, brought a smile to my face, and probably more importantly, it put my mind at ease, allowing it to wander to matters related to the case.

There was nothing of note in the warehouse.

No evidence that anyone had used it in years before the last couple of nights. There was an old television, a couch, and a light hooked up to a diesel generator. There was sure to be DNA in the room, but I didn't have access to that technology, nor did I have the time to chase it. It was clear that someone had used the room, but there was no evidence as to who that might've been. Nothing was left behind, if there had ever been much there in the first place.

We didn't even know if it was Millie in the garage. It could've been a coincidence. Squatters could've heard us coming, and then made a run for it once we were too close. That was certainly a possibility as there was nothing in the room to say that a girl had been there, less so that Millie herself had been present.

We spent much of the night looking for any connections between the 'Top-Notch Service Garage' and our main suspects, but we came up short. All avenues led nowhere. There was nothing that could point us in a particular direction. Ruby Jones's father was a mechanic, but he had no connections to the 'Top-Notch Service Garage.'

The van was empty. And white. The correct color, but then the color white on a van was as common as the color blonde on a dolly bird at the Playboy Mansion.

I opened my phone and looked at the picture of Millie again—pigtails in her hair, broad smile on her face. So sweet, so innocent, and so free. The thought that Millie was in the back of the car that raced past us meant that I couldn't sleep. Who would even think of doing that to a little girl? What heartless soul would do that?

How could anyone ever harm an innocent child?

It took me back to thoughts about Alannah, my niece. Just after Alannah was born, Claire dragged me all the way down to the lawyer's office to make me sign a will. When Claire drafted hers, two years before she died, she made sure that there was money left behind for her niece, so that she was looked after and could benefit should anything happen to us, her extended family. The fact that Ben took that money, took Claire's legacy and generous gift, and gambled it on a risky investment made me angry. Real angry.

My hand gripped the edge of the seat tighter, thinking about how Alannah would never know or benefit from what Claire had selflessly done for her, or even know about it. She'd know about her deceased aunty but not that her aunty went the extra mile for her and had her back.

Ben was an idiot, and his sister knew that he would mess things up along the way. Sure enough, he had, and he was now talking about bankruptcy, which also meant that he could lose his job as a police officer.

"You look like you're thinking. That must hurt."

It was Derrick Booth; a retired cop, but not a retired smartass, and owner of Barclay, a fellow golden retriever.

"I was thinking about my wife's favorite joke. Wanna hear it?"

"May she rest in peace." Despite being in his seventies, Derrick always had a thing for my wife. He flirted with her at the dog park whenever she took Winston for a run. There was an awkward silence for a moment, before Derrick went on. "Well, come on then, out with it."

"My favorite pen writes underwater." I paused for a few moments. "It writes lots of other words as well, but underwater is a nice word to write."

Derrick laughed. "She was a school teacher, wasn't she?"

"She was."

"Well, I've got a more mature joke for you—my friend took a Viagra yesterday, but it got stuck in his throat. Poor guy had a stiff neck all day."

We laughed together.

Derrick Booth basically owned the bench at the east end of the dog park. For the last ten years, he'd sat on the bench more than he had his own couch. When his wife passed away, this became his social outlet, hour after hour sitting on the bench. His wife had spent much of her forty-five years organizing his social life, and when she passed, he felt lost, alone, and empty. The park gave him an outlet, a chance to make friends out of strangers. Booth was the hub of the park, the person anyone could talk to, the social connection that a lot of people yearned for. As for me, I could take him in small doses, I wasn't after a social connection when I came here, just fresh air and time spent with Winston. But today was different. Today I was actively searching him out.

A little overweight, he was in his late seventies, and his tanned face would've been handsome once, perhaps half a century ago. Now it was sort of interesting, a bit like a beat-up old sports car that would have once been cutting edge but now was just kind of novel.

He sat next to me on the bench, watching as his dog chased after mine. The park was almost empty with only one other dog running around, along the grass that was patchy at best, the result of too much digging from our canine friends. The chain fence that surrounded the park wouldn't hold many dogs back, if they really wanted to run through it, and the trees looked tired, as if they were ready to give up any moment. Still, the air was fresh and we were outdoors so it was good enough for me.

"Did you hear about Hugh Guthrie's case?" Booth questioned. "Been all over the news this morning. They threw it out."

"I heard."

"It was a technicality. Something wrong with the way that Guthrie was arrested. I don't know the full details. All I know is that a killer gets to walk free because someone somewhere didn't do something by the book." Booth sighed. "And a killer walks back onto the street."

My fists clenched tight, my jaw ground together, and my vision focused on a faraway point. I was trying hard to calm the rage. Hugh Guthrie had walked free.

The justice that Claire deserved, the justice I needed, was taken away from me.

I didn't respond to Booth. Instead, I stood and paced the dog park, mumbling to myself. I punched a fence along the way, letting out steam.

Guthrie had walked free. I couldn't believe it. The system had failed me. The system had failed the memory of my Claire.

After five minutes of pacing the yard, I came back to the bench to sit next to Booth. I couldn't get distracted. Not now. Guthrie would have to wait.

"Sorry I bought the case up," Booth stated. "So what were you thinking about that's causing you to look like you're constipated?"

"A case."

"Sometimes it helps to think out loud. Give me the low down on it, Valentine. Share the burden and halve it with me."

I could sense the excitement in his voice, as much as he tried to hide it this was clearly the most intrigue he'd had for some time. When you've spent the best part of forty years investigating crime as a former detective, it's hard to leave it behind.

"I have a crime that I'm trying to solve without getting the police involved. Everything has to be done behind the scenes and kept quiet."

He looked out at the park and nodded, as if he was only half listening.

"Kidnapping?"

"Why do you say that?"

He shrugged. "It's about the only crime that the victims don't want the police involved in. Or, more accurately, the perpetrators are insistent that the police aren't involved in. But as an ex-cop my advice every time is go to the police, sure they make mistakes from time to time, but given their resources, they're the best bet statistically. And I say that from experience, Jack."

I didn't respond.

After a few minutes of silence, it was clear Derrick couldn't resist digging a bit further. Not that I could blame him, and he had enough experience to be potentially of use to me.

"Who are your suspects?"

"Mechanics, or possibly relatives of mechanics."

"Interesting." He rubbed his chin. "Want to know what I think?"

The real answer was 'yes' but I was reluctant to let Derrick know that I valued his opinion. If I did I'd never hear the end of it, so I answered with a non-committal sounding 'maybe,' as if, in actual fact, I preferred a bit of silence with my own thoughts so they could organize themselves, but that I would listen to the old guy anyway out of respect or simple social convention.

"Mechanics are a tight knit bunch, but they also have a group of people around the outside of them." He raised his finger. "If you can't find a connection to a mechanic, then I would say look to the people around the mechanics."

I groaned inwardly; he was starting to sound like a vague mystic karate instructor.

"I've looked at their families," I replied, more in an attempt to get him to furnish me with something concrete and specific than to encourage him.

"No, no." He shook his head and his chin wobbled as well. "Not families. You need to look for someone like a truck driver."

That got my attention. "Truck driver?"

"Auto enthusiasts do most of their own work, so they don't need mechanics. The closest people to mechanics are the people that need their vehicles for work. Truck drivers or delivery drivers. That's who you need to be looking at."

His statement hit me.

I hated to admit it, but he was right.

CHAPTER 12

KYLE WATERS wasn't hard to track down. In fact, it was downright easy to find him.

A few phone calls to his employers, under a fake name, of course, and I was told where he had parked his hauler for the night. Traveling from North Dakota to Tennessee, hauling a semi full of brand-new expensive furniture to satisfy the population's ongoing urge to spend ever more money, Kyle regularly found himself a resident at the Iowa 80 Truck stop, sleeping there in the spacious cabin of his semi.

A Disneyland for truck lovers, the Iowa 80 was three hours outside of Chicago, and had the title of the World's Largest Truck Stop. Quite a title, but as I drove into the complex, I saw that this wasn't just a truck stop, this was more like a mini-city, complete with amenities, services, repair shops and even a trucker's museum—not that I had the time or inclination to go in there. But more than the buildings, more than the shops, I found that this was also a community hub, a place for those traveling the lonely hours on the road to congregate and talk about their journey. Here they could find human comradery and contact after hours of solitary confinement on the open road. They could plug back into a community, of sorts, and find solace there after all that time alone where they only had the workings of their own mind, or the radio, for company.

With more than nine hundred parking spots for trucks, the food court was constantly busy, satisfying the urges of the hard-working truckers, who could then work off the excess in the gym only a few feet away—not that too many of them did, however, going by the abundance of oversized guts on display as I walked around, but I was reliably informed that my target never missed an opportunity to work out.

And so, that was where I found Kyle, pumping iron after another long and monotonous haul. He was aggressively grunting as I stepped into the small gym, located on the third floor of the main building in the truck stop. Dressed in a yellow tank top, shorts and sneakers, the muscles were clear to see.

I had done my research on Kyle, and it was clear that his years in the army had left their mark—down his right arm, that is, where a long battle-hardened scar was clear to see.

He grunted as I stepped in, and I did the same. He lifted, I lifted. He stretched, I stretched. I was mirroring his actions, important to create trust between us. I lifted weights, and although I could've, throughout the half-an-hour workout, I made a point of never lifting heavier weights than his.

I was lucky that I looked the part as well—I had stopped by a second hand shop on the drive to the truck stop, purchasing a complete outfit of ripped shorts, old sneakers, and a Metallica t-shirt, for under five dollars. I wondered what Casey would think, she was always on my case about my style, in fact, she was always on my case, period, but today's outfit really did look like I was in dire need of an emergency fashion make-over.

"What are you hauling?" After thirty minutes, Kyle finally broke the silence.

"Furniture." I wiped my brow. "You?"

"Same. I'm hauling a whole bunch of tables from a workshop in North Dakota to a showroom in Nashville."

I nodded in a way that implied that was the sort of jobs I was used to.

"Do you make that run often?"

"About twice a month they get me to haul it. It's expensive stuff too, each table's worth over ten grand. Can you believe that? Who spends ten grand on a table?" He smiled. "I would much rather spend that money on beer."

"Ten grand on beer? That would last at least the weekend at my place."

We laughed. That was good. The bond was building.

He was a big guy, broad shouldered, with thick

arms. His black hair was cropped short and his beard was two-day old stubble. His skin was weathered, and his eyes looked like they had seen death too many times.

"When did you start the run?" I asked.

"This morning. I've been on the road ten hours. Was in Chicago before that."

"Yeah, not far off that myself today."

The timeline fit for the escape from the warehouse.

"Running by yourself?" I continued.

"This time, yeah."

"I brought my kid with me last time," I lied. I was pushing for information, and building a bond. "It was a shorter run. He's only six but he enjoyed the hours on the road. He loves sleeping in the cabin, thinks it's camping or something, sort of an oversized cubby house, doesn't realize that after a while the novelty wears off good and proper and there is nothing better than leaving it all behind and sleeping in your own bed. You got kids?"

"I've got a twenty-year old son in Detroit from my first marriage, and a five-year-old stepdaughter in Chicago from my second marriage."

"Going around twice? That must be expensive." I laughed but he flinched. That hit a nerve.

"It sure is expensive. Sometimes I wonder how we're going to make ends meet." He sighed. "The stepdaughter's father is mega rich, the type of guy that would buy a ten grand table and never use it. In fact, he'd probably buy a couple."

We both shook our heads at that idea.

"Still, must make bringing up the kid easier."

"But that's the thing," He wiped his brow with his gym towel. "The guy doesn't pay a cent. My wife signed a pre-nup with him, so he pays nothing. We're almost broke, trying to survive paycheck to paycheck, and that prick lives in a fancy penthouse, drives several fancy cars, and vacations all around the world."

"What about child support? He's gotta pay something towards you bringing up his little brat."

Kyle gave me a sharp look.

"Nah, his fancy lawyers got it all worked out for him, he has no clue how much it really costs to bring up a kid, especially with him insisting she wears designer clothes when she stays with him."

He took a swig from his water bottle before continuing.

"Still, she's a sweet kid, you know. I'd do anything for her and her mom. They deserve a lot better." Kyle trailed off as if thinking about something more. "But I'm doing my best for them."

"Doesn't seem fair."

That brought him back.

"You want to talk about fair? How about the fact that I risked my life for this country, the blessed United States of America, and leave with nothing, and all that guy does is rip people off and he gets to live the fancy life. That's not fair."

I'd definitely hit a nerve.

"Those politicians have something to answer for." I quipped.

"Nah, not them. I have great respect for my country and its leaders. The greatest country on the planet, no question about it—not that I've been to any others, but then why in God's name would you need to?" He chuckled to himself. "This country was founded on ideals of hard work and rewards, where anyone could be successful if you just work at it."

I moved towards his bag. I could see his keys sitting inside the zipper of the bag. He was distracted as he continued to talk about his life, the world, and everything in between so I decided to take the risk.

"But they forgot to factor in the snakes. Snakes like Chase Martin." Kyle spat out the last words with total disgust, like it hurt him to even utter them.

Pretending to stretch my hamstring, I leaned forward, and with one quick motion, I reached inside his bag and deftly swiped his keys, pocketing them inside my shorts.

"That man is a con artist, he conned his way to money and power, he conned my Tanya and even cons his own little girl. Just another scumbag who'd do anything to get to the top."

"That's the world," I said, as I moved the keys from my pocket into my gym bag. "It'd be hard to change it."

"We just need to go back to the way things were. Back to the American way. We have to stop all this progress and just settle down."

"Well, you're right about that," I replied, trying to get back on the same wavelength.

He was proud of his country, an honorable guy, I could tell that right away. I changed the subject quickly before he got any more off track.

"Which truck you hauling with?"

"A red 2015 Kenworth. Recently, I had flames painted down the side."

"Nice. Big cabin?"

"You bet. It's parked out back."

Good. I had the truck. If he had the girl, then it would be easy to find out if she was holed up inside there.

"I'm going to hit the showers, but it was good to meet you." He held out his hand. "I'm Kyle."

"Jack." He held out his hand to shake. I grasped a palm which was rough like sandpaper. He had big, coarse, working hands, not like the prissy manicured hands of Chase Martin, but the real thing, a real man's hand. We shook and his grip felt like it could crush a watermelon.

He stepped out to the showers and I ran outside to find his truck.

If the girl was there, I was sure she'd be safe.

I found myself hoping she was there. Kyle cared

about Millie, and he was too honorable to hurt a child. It would have been the perfect scenario, a quick and easy conclusion.

Sometimes cases are solved quickly and easily, but in my experience those are rare indeed. Most often they are long and messy and people get hurt along the way.

I looked in his truck and found nothing, no sign of the girl, before handing the keys back into the front desk, saying that he'd left them in the gym.

Kyle was still a suspect—he had the means to take the girl—and the motive too, although he clearly didn't have her with him, that didn't preclude the possibility that he was holding Millie elsewhere.

<u>CHAPTER 13</u>

GENERALLY SPEAKING, I hated the modern phone apps.

But I must admit, there was something appealing about using them that I found hard to resist. There was a highly addictive nature to them and once hooked they could be really hard to quit. They became a habit, often used without a conscious decision to do so.

Casey was always trying out the latest apps, research she said, but I knew it was her way of letting her brain relax and go someplace other than work, to put that stress on hold, at least for a while.

Why she had to share them with me though, I didn't know.

The latest fad was an app that showed what children would look like based on uploading another person's face into it – either a real person you know or, more often than not, a fantasy celebrity. It then mixed up a selection of facial features from both your picture and the other person and, voila! Out popped an offspring. I'd heard about it, I'd seen others using it—often resulting in a lot of laughter—and up until this point I'd done my best to resist it.

But sometimes resistance is futile.

Casey had tried it with Ed Sheeran, Damian Lewis and even Prince Harry, apparently she had a bit of a thing for ginger haired Englishmen, and she was pretty happy with the results. And for a laugh she paired me with Beyoncé, Hillary Clinton and the Queen of England, but I didn't stick around for the results. My chance for kids had gone. Gone with Claire.

But sitting in my office, with two days down, just three days to go, Millie's disappearance was weighing heavily on my mind, and I couldn't resist downloading the app. I uploaded a picture of my face, I'd like to say a good picture of my face but then in truth they ranged from bad to not quite so bad, and then I uploaded a picture of Claire's face. Any picture would do, Claire always looked beautiful; was beautiful, inside and out: face like an angel and a heart like a saint.

And dammit, the picture of our potential offspring was gorgeous.

But more than that, more than the features, was the fact that our downloaded offspring looked like she could be a cousin of Millie Martin. Blonde hair, blue eyes, soft smile. So damn cute. Clearly the app used more of Claire's photo than mine.

I had to do everything I could to protect that child. I couldn't let her be hurt, or that would weigh on my mind for the rest of my life.

I'd already lost Claire. I couldn't afford to lose Millie as well.

Something shifted inside of me, a subtle change in my perception of things. A determination to find Millie, to save Millie, no matter what, began to take ahold of me as if she were my very own child, Claire's own child, the daughter we never had.

Turning off the app, I looked around my office. It was just as well that we didn't have a child before Claire was taken from me, I couldn't imagine a child growing up in this world. My world was filled with crimes, hatred and anger, and there was no way to avoid it. But Millie was real and alive somewhere. The thought of her fear and possible suffering ate a hole in me. I was going to rescue her and to take down anyone who got in my way, so help me God.

This was the only work I knew, the only thing I was good at, and the thought of giving it up to work in a respectable office would've killed me. I couldn't imagine sitting in front of a computer for hours on end, slugging away on a keyboard to make money for someone else's business.

However, an office job would've been a thousand times better than a customer service role. I would be lucky to last a morning before I got fired. If there was one thing I hated, it was when people complained. Worse still was the thought of smiling meekly in response to a customers' complaints. I liked to hit back, both figuratively and literally. I wouldn't be able to hold back on my advice about where these people could file their complaints.

I opened a news website. Another kid missing in Florida. The FBI said that they were copycats, and had high hopes of getting the child back this time. I didn't have any hope for that kid. If the gangs were evil enough to kidnap a child, then they were evil enough to pull the trigger. They weren't messing around, and fear was spreading through the country. 'Keep your kids safe,' the Governor said. 'Don't let them wander the streets alone.'

I read the article on the kidnapping and then turned to the local news on the site. Hugh Guthrie made a headline. He would love that.

The article talked about the lack of justice for newscaster Brian Gates, who Guthrie murdered. There had to be another way to get Guthrie. There had to be another way to get justice.

I heard Chase before I saw him. He stormed through the door into my office, the fear running through his movements.

"She's run away." He stepped into my office. "She's gone."

I paused for a moment before I responded. "Who are we talking about?"

"Ruby. My girlfriend."

"Right. Did you ask her where Millie was?"

"Ask her? Ask her?!" He slammed his hand on my

desk. "This isn't the time for asking!"

"You accused her of hurting Millie?" My voice was calm, a perfect foil to his anger.

"I said that I knew she had Millie and I needed to know where she was." He began to pace the room in front of my desk, head turning this way and that, clearly agitated. "She said she had no idea what I was talking about, and then she started saying that she was going to be famous, and was going to move all the way to LA to be with some big shot there."

If it wasn't for Millie, I would have laughed.

"For a movie producer?"

"That's it. Some guy she met near a coffee shop. She's so gullible. I told her that the movie producer just wanted to sleep with her, that he didn't see any potential in her other than her physical attributes and that she was a fool if she got caught up in all his lies."

"And then?"

"And then she stormed out and said that Millie had destroyed our relationship."

"What did she mean by that?"

Chase gave a frustrated sigh.

"It was her stupid little dream of me taking her to LA so she could have her shot at being a star. I would let her have her fantasy, smile and nod, agree how amazing it would be, but I never intended to go through with it, and she was slowly starting to figure that out. Ruby blamed it on Millie, but the truth is, I'm just not interested. The woman has no talent beyond taking photographs of herself. She's a vacuous little airhead who looks good. Take that away and she's nothing. Ruby and I won't last, I'll get bored, already am, really, and then I'll move on. And when I leave Chicago, it will be somewhere chosen by me, not a girlfriend or anyone else."

"What about Millie?"

"Millie?" Chase looked genuinely confused. "She's a kid, she doesn't get a say. What's any of this got to do with it anyway, we've got to track down Ruby!"

"Any idea where she went?" I asked.

"I don't know." Chase ran his hand through his hair. "I have no idea where she went. I tried to follow her, but she started screaming as soon as we got on the street. I tried to grab her, but some guy stepped between us, probably trying to act like the tough guy in front of a pretty girl, and she got into a cab. And now she won't answer my calls."

"Not at home?"

"I called her home and her mother answered, but she said she hadn't seen Ruby. She said Ruby and her father have been acting strange lately. She didn't know where Ruby's father was either. He's got mob connections, Jack. He's got a lot of connections in that world." He turned to me. "This is your fault. You told me it was Ruby."

"I didn't tell you it was Ruby."

"It's your fault." He waved his finger near my face, leaning across my desk. "I shouldn't have hired you."

"I suggest you put that finger down before I snap it off like a dry twig."

My calm demeanor caught him off-guard. He expected me to shout and scream, get into a verbal duel, but that wasn't my way. I was a man of action, not of talk.

"I can't let her hurt Millie, Jack."

A rare glimpse of parental care. Time for a bit of the good cop routine, soften him up.

"We're not going to let that happen, but we have to get prepared. And that means no more going off like a loose cannon. You came to me because you knew I was your best hope. You've got to trust me now."

He turned away from me, and started pacing the room again. "What am I going to do?"

"Focus on what we can do. How is the money going?"

"I've got it. All of it is ready to go. I just need to pick it up from the bank, it's not as easy as visiting an ATM for an amount like this. I have an appointment with the manager to collect it this afternoon. Then I'll keep it in my safe at home. The whole building is under tight security. I've told the security team to be extra vigilant over the next few days, although I didn't tell them why. I trust them, but I don't trust anyone that much."

He paced the room for a few more moments, before sitting in the chair opposite me. He slumped like a depressed teenager, seemingly powerless to affect his world.

"Now I need you to think, Chase. Is there anyone else that you think could've taken Millie? Anyone else that comes to mind? Someone you've overlooked, perhaps?"

"What? Are you telling me that Ruby didn't do it?" He sat forward.

"I never told you that she did. I told you she was a suspect, the same as all the other people are at the moment. I'm investigating all the leads, but so far, we have nothing concrete."

"I don't want to lose that million dollars."

"What about Millie?"

The question shocked him. "Of course, I don't want to lose Millie either."

"There are still some leads that we need to follow, but we're getting closer." I opened a file. "Is there anyone you know that's a mechanic or connected to a mechanic?"

"Mechanic?"

"That's where the clues are leading."

"Ruby's father was a mechanic, although he's been retired for years. But I have no clue where they are now."

"I need you to try and find out where they might've gone. Go and see Ruby's mother at her house, and tell me the second you hear anything." I didn't feel it was a strong possibility, but the option was still open. I tapped my fingers on the side of the table. "Where do you get your cars serviced?"

"I have them serviced at a dealership. I don't know the mechanics' names, I only deal with the receptionist, but I'm sure they don't have anything to with it. That shop wouldn't do this sort of thing." He thought for a few moments. "Why do you say it's a mechanic?"

"It could be nothing, but that's where the clues are leading."

He stared at the table, and I could almost see the thoughts going through his head.

"And," he stated, "There's also Damon. Millie's grandfather."

"What about him?"

"He's a former mechanic. Worked hard his whole life and has nothing to show for it because he didn't work smart." Chase looked up. "And he's always been jealous of my money, the way I've done well."

"I thought you said he was the only member of Tanya's family that you still got along with?"

Chase shifted uncomfortably.

"Things have been a bit tense since the last investment went south. And he's been especially cold since Ruby came on the scene. We had a bit of a fight about it. I think he finally realized Tanya and I were finished." Chase ran his hand through his hair again, before continuing. "He said Millie would be better off without me, that Ruby was a bad influence and that I was only good for my money."

Chase leaned forward and looked me in the eyes, he was angry now.

"And then he said I wasn't even much good for that, what I pay each month doesn't cover Millie's food, let alone anything else, and he hopes I had some trust fund set up for Millie's future. How dare he! I worked my way up from nothing and then people expect me to share it around like a charity. Well, I told him what I thought of that. And I told him that he and all the other blue-collar poor only had themselves to blame."

Chase let out an angry breath and relaxed, slumped back into the chair.

I waited, I could tell Chase had something more to get off his chest.

Chase sighed before speaking again.

"Maybe he's right. Maybe Millie is better off without me. But could he really be behind this? He's an old man, and he's sick…" Chase trailed off.

"I don't know," I responded. "But it's my job to find out."

CHAPTER 14

I HATED ties.

None seemed to fit my neck. Not that I looked like an offensive lineman, but my neck was solid. The jacket felt even worse. My shoulders didn't feel free, and I felt like if I moved the wrong way, the entire suit would rip apart.

"Don't look so rigid," Casey smiled as we stepped out of the car. "You need to look more natural."

"More natural? This is about as unnatural as I get." I ran my finger along the collar of my shirt. "I could never work in an office."

"Nobody would want you to work in their office. I've heard you type on your computer keyboard. You're like a caveman thumping a stone tablet with a club."

"Thanks." I managed a grin. "So this is it?"

"This is where Damon said we could find him." Casey looked up at the building. "Said he was going to be here all day."

The American Veteran's Club was a small building in the west of Logan Square, an area I knew well. Casey contacted Damon under the guise that we were school workers and had received an enrollment for Millie at a new Catholic school and Damon had been listed as a reference.

The building was busy, it was just after lunch time, and the volunteers at the center had just served lunch for around two hundred men and women. I liked these places. These were the places that supported returned service men and women, let them tell their stories, let them know that they were not alone, that there was someone there who would listen and help.

From what we found, we knew that Damon was very active in the community, be that with veterans, the center for the homeless, or helping out the aged community by doing odd-jobs around their homes. An all-around good guy. Or so it seemed on the surface. I needed to dig deeper, to look beneath the veneer and find out if there was another side to him, a darker side kept hidden from public view – a side that could kidnap a young girl from her parents.

We found him in the kitchen, working hard scrubbing dishes, laughing with his fellow kitchen hands. With our business attire, we didn't fit in well.

We introduced ourselves, Damon excused himself from the kitchen, wiped his hands on a towel and led us to the small dining room at the side of the larger hall where most people were seated. There were rows of former servicemen and women all eating their meals together, some talking and laughing, others somber and reserved but all together breaking bread in solidarity. It was a sight that gladdened the heart.

He glanced over the form that we gave him, including his address and any details that we might have missed before.

"So that's why you were at Chase's apartment the other day," stated Damon, "I knew you weren't a friend of his when we first met. You were more casually dressed then."

"That's right. We were talking about the enrollment."

"He said that you were doing work for him?"

"Let's just say, it's a competitive business, getting into good schools, these days." I gave Damon a knowing look and moved on before he could think about it too much. "Please do have a good look at the form."

He glanced back at the paperwork.

"My daughter didn't tell me about this," he said with a touch of suspicion. "Can Chase do that? Just enroll a child in a new school without the mother's permission?"

"I assure you, we need both parents to sign the paperwork for enrollment," Casey calmed his nerves as she shut the door behind us. "We don't need to be a part of any family conflict," she added with a little laugh.

"However, we are not at the enrollment stage just yet," Casey continued, serious again. "Our Lady of St. Mary's is a small school providing the best education money can buy, and I'm sure you can appreciate we have a large number of applications each year. So this is just an informal meeting to ensure we are the right school for Millie."

"Our Lady of St. Mary's, you say?" He rubbed his brow. "I've never heard of that school and I've been around this area for many, many years."

"We're still new, two years old, but we're growing in both numbers and reputation. We need to make sure that we have only the best children at our school, so that Millie can be assured that she will learn and socialize not just with high achievers but also those with strong Catholic values."

Damon still looked doubtful.

"And Chase put me down as a reference on the form?"

"He did," I responded, looking around. "We can already see you are an active member of your community. Now, do you mind if we ask you some questions?"

Damon nodded.

The room was small—kitchen to one side, a fridge in the corner, and a table with five mismatched chairs. We sat down, and Casey opened a file with Millie's photo attached. She was doing a very good job of presenting herself as a member of a Catholic school recruitment team. Even I was convinced as she provided Damon a run-down about the school.

"So now, can you tell us a little about your

background first?" Casey asked.

"I'm a war vet. Served in Iraq back in the early nineties, retired after two tours, and went into my father's trade, which was a mechanic. Did that for most of my life. I retired from work ten years ago, just after the death of my wife, and I've spent the last decade doing a lot of volunteering. I work in the kitchen here, mow lawns for elderly people who can't do it themselves, and feed the homeless with the soup van that runs around here. Lots of different things, mostly organized through my church, St. Michael's, but just trying to help people."

Casey nodded approvingly.

"Sounds like a very colorful life."

"Well, I worked hard, slaved away for decades, although I don't have much else to show for it. Chase is the one with money. I suppose I should be glad of that, for Millie's sake. She will have opportunities I could never have given Tanya, her mother. I risked my life for this country, and did five decades of honest work, and I'm not left with much. Don't even own my house. Lost it when my business went under. But people like Chase know how to make money. That's what he's good at."

Damon was getting off track, if this was a real interview, I wouldn't like Millie's chances of getting in, but it was providing a useful insight for us. Still, we didn't want to lose our plausibility, so I shot Casey a look to get the interview back on course.

"And what can you tell us about Millie? Is she calm, energetic, or very expressive? What are her interests and talents?" Casey sat with a pen ready to take notes. "Anything you can tell us about her will be helpful."

"Millie is the sweetest, cutest, nicest girl you'll ever meet. Her smile radiates around the room, her blue eyes are so innocent, and her laugh, well, her laugh makes me laugh." Damon stopped to think for a moment. "She loves to sing," he continued. "Got that talent from her Grandma Ruth, God rest her soul," Damon made the sign of the cross. "Ruth would be proud of her, though she never met her. Millie is sweet natured, just like Ruth used to be. She's an angel, I'm sure of that. They both are, one in heaven and one on earth." He shook his head. "I'm just sad that I won't be around to see the woman that she becomes."

Neither Casey nor I responded. How could we? What do you say to a man who's just admitted that his days are numbered?

"I have cancer, you see." After a long pause, he continued. "I don't have long left, and I've done just about all I can for Millie here on earth. I'll be up in heaven soon, but at least I know that Millie is provided for, I've made sure of that."

If Damon was our kidnapper, he was on the verge of saying too much, but was too caught up in his plan to realize. One gentle nudge and he might just spill the information we needed.

"Yes, it must be reassuring to know her father has the means to provide for her."

I was banking on him not wanting Chase to get the credit.

Damon frowned at me for a moment, slightly confused. "No, not Chase." He looked down at his hands with a nod, "I'm going to leave something special behind for her when I go."

"Ah," I nodded approvingly, "a legacy trust fund." I was pushing for a more specific answer.

"I'm sorry." He looked up from the table and took a deep breath. "I shouldn't be so depressed about these things. I've lived a great life, and my wife is up there in heaven waiting for me. That's why I've been volunteering, you see." He joked. "So I can get into heaven with the wife."

Damon looked back down at the paperwork. "So, I guess I'd better get this filled in for you."

"Thank you, just a few minor details, in case we need to get in touch again." Casey answered as she tidied up her notes.

"It's a good legacy to leave behind," Casey said reassuringly, but shot me a look while Damon was busy writing and I could tell she thought I had pushed too hard. "All this volunteering that you do, we can see that Millie comes from a good family. It will certainly help us while we process the application."

Damon handed over his form and Casey closed

the folder. "Thank you for your time."

After shaking his hand, we left the building, not saying a word until we entered the truck.

Once we closed the doors, I looked at Casey and could see she shared my thoughts.

"We have a new suspect."

CHAPTER 15

THE STREET was quiet, as was the apartment building.

Damon rented a one-bedroom apartment on the third floor of a Logan Square apartment block, a far cry from the house that he used to own and live in. The financial crisis was not kind to him. He lost his family home, his business, and all of his retirement plan.

After the loss of his wife, he was left with nothing. Not a cent to his name after a life of hard work.

Casey scoped out the third floor first, and when she didn't find any activity, I followed her, scoping for cameras as I went. There were none, not that I expected to find any. Damon had mentioned that he would be at the Veterans Club until after 5pm, so we had time to have a thorough look around.

After a quick jimmy of the door lock, it swung wide open. Locks aren't too hard to pick, if you know what you're doing, that is, especially older ones. One simple twist with two pins, and the door pops open, with a little bit of practice, of course. And I'd done plenty over the years. I'd started early, over twenty years ago, with a simple 'how to' book on the subject and had progressed through all the various picking tools and innovations as they were developed and came on the market. Oftentimes when I sat watching the television, I'd be practicing on a new lock mechanism, working away at it with the tools of the trade until I could crack it in moments. It used to drive Claire bananas.

We stepped in quietly, hoping to find the television on, and Millie watching it safe and well.

There was one couch, faced towards the old television, one small wooden dining table, two chairs, and a sparsely filled kitchen. The bedroom and bathroom were the same—spotlessly cleaned, dustless, and perfectly ordered.

There were a group of children's books on the bookshelf, toys in a box next to the television, and boxes of children's breakfast cereal in the cupboard, but no sign that Millie was currently staying there.

"I've got nothing." Casey walked into the kitchen where I was looking through a drawer. "Not even a bill to a new place."

"I'm the same," I replied, banging the drawer closed with frustration. "Nothing to indicate that he was planning this, nothing to show that he researched it, and nothing to show that he has any connections to any old repair shops."

Casey sighed sympathetically.

"Wrong guy?"

"Maybe." I shrugged. "But I'm not wiping him off the list yet. He has the motive to do this."

We checked once more through all the drawers, looking for a bill or a notice of rent for another place, anything that might suggest he had somewhere else to keep Millie, but again, we came up short.

Casey gave up and flopped down onto the sofa.

"There's nothing here, Jack. What's our next move?"

At that moment, we heard a knock on the apartment door.

We froze, our eyes locking on to the door.

"Damon, is that you?" An elderly woman's voice called out. "Damon? I heard noises from your apartment, and you haven't been around this week. And you haven't returned my calls."

We didn't respond, barely moving, barely breathing.

She knocked again.

"You've missed the rent again this week." The lady called out. "You've got until Friday to pay it. I know things are tight, but you can't keep missing rent. I've been reasonable with you and I want to help, really I do, but I can't give you beyond Friday, ok? This time it has to be paid, in full. Otherwise I've got no choice but to pursue eviction. I don't want to do that. I don't want you out on the street. But I'm not a charity either, understand? I still have bills to pay."

Casey and I looked at each other. Financial

troubles were certainly on his list of motives.

When we heard the light footsteps walk back down the hall, we exhaled.

"Let's wrap this up," I whispered to Casey. "Get out before she comes back with the keys."

Quietly, we snuck back out of the building, taking the stairs and out the back entrance.

We walked to my truck parked a block away, our minds too busy racing through the possible scenarios to discuss it out loud.

We got in and sat quietly in the truck, not going anywhere, not talking, just staring into the nothingness.

"Do you think they'll hurt her?" Casey finally broke the silence.

"I don't know." My hand gripped the steering wheel. "I don't even want to think about it. That innocent girl doesn't deserve any pain."

I banged my fist on the steering wheel, causing Casey to jump.

"I really thought we were on the right track, first Kyle, then Damon, but we keep coming up empty handed. We've got to start considering other possibilities."

Casey snapped out of her melancholy mood and got into brainstorming.

"Come on Jack, let's talk through this. I feel we're close too. We just need to find a new angle."

Casey pulled out her tablet and flicked open her

notes.

"Ok, what if the kidnapper is unrelated to Chase? Someone just saw an opportunity and took it?"

I shook my head.

"It's too planned, too well thought out for that. This isn't opportunistic. It's premeditated."

Casey nodded.

"Professionals then? They're in the news a lot. Maybe it's a gang that wants to take advantage of the news. It wouldn't have taken much to find Chase as a target. He's an easy pick. Loads of people know he's got money, hell, he flashes the cash around enough."

"If they're professionals, then they won't let Millie live." I took my phone out and stared at the picture of Millie. "And I won't let them hurt her. Anybody hurts her and they die."

"All I'm saying is that we have to look at other possibilities. Time is running out. If the drop doesn't go well, or they are professionals, then Millie won't make it out of this."

I could see what Casey was trying to do, and bit by bit her pep talk was working.

"You're right. Let's think this through, every angle."

I was back in detective mode. Back on the scent. And ready to track down the target.

"Have your contacts mentioned anything about kidnapping gangs?"

"Nothing. You?"

"My contacts are the same, and I think that if a new gang came into the city, people would already be talking. What about the last groups of people that he tried to rip off?"

"There's not a lot of information about them, but from what I've found, he's more likely to choose larger investment firms who need to sweep this sort of bad investment under the carpet. This was the first time that he's targeted a smaller group of individuals."

"I'd say that the investment funds had caught onto his fraudulent schemes. Word travels quickly in those circles, and they would've known to steer clear of him."

"Then who else do we have?"

We stared out of the truck for a while.

"Remind me again, who else was on the list of people who were ripped off by Chase's most recent display of moral goodness?" I questioned.

Casey scrolled through her notes again.

"Two of the people on the list have since died. James Peterson committed suicide not long after losing the money, no partner, no kids, parents deceased, so no one left behind to look for revenge. And David Malone, died of a heart attack before the investment went under. His wife has been in Canada with her family ever since. As far as I could tell, she didn't even know about the money."

Casey scrolled on.

"Another four were elderly, all without family and

127

pretty frail, couldn't kidnap a mouse. Two of them didn't even know the money was gone when I spoke to them."

I shook my head in disgust. "Chase certainly did his homework."

"Next two are still in the armed forces, currently on deployment and out of the country at the time of the kidnapping. Again, not a lot of family to speak of. One from a troubled background, seems to have cut all ties with whatever family he had, the other is originally from Florida and any family is still there. Both unmarried."

"Could either of them have planned it from there, arranged for someone to do it for them?"

Casey shook her head, "I don't think so. I tried to get in touch with them but apparently they are unreachable at the moment."

Casey closed her tablet and looked at me with a shrug.

"Which leaves?" I asked, even though I was fairly sure of the answer.

"From the list of investors? Kyle, the trucker, and your brother-in-law, Ben." Casey put her tablet away. "Do you think Tanya knew that Kyle had lost that money?"

"Yeah, I'm sure she would've known. They seem like the sort of couple that wouldn't keep secrets from each other. When was Kyle due back in the city?"

"This afternoon. Do you need me to put a tail on

them?"

"That's a very good idea. Him and the wife."

Casey put her seatbelt on and looked at me.

"I've been thinking about this, and Chase is the real bad guy here. He's the one ripping people off and betraying their trust. Karma has a way of coming to people who deserve it."

"Doesn't make this the right way to get revenge. Two wrongs don't make a right."

"But three lefts do." She smiled as I tried to work that response over in my head. "All I'm saying is that Chase deserves something bad to happen to him. He deserves someone to come after him."

"But Millie doesn't." I roared the truck into life. "She's innocent, and I'm not going to let anyone hurt her."

CHAPTER 16

SOME PEOPLE are easy to follow.

They live their lives in the routine bubble of everyday life. They walk the same route, look at the same things in the same way, and generally move through the motions without even looking twice. Only something really dramatic makes an impact in their zombie-like world. It's easy to blend into the background and watch those people, those who dwell in the land of the living dead. The danger when following them is not to become complacent. You still have to remain alert and tail them as if they were super vigilant. Sometimes when something is too easy you let your guard down. And when you let your guard down you miss something that under normal circumstances would never get past you.

Tanya walked to her car after her shift had finished at the bar. She had a hard look on her face. Tough and uncompromising. A look that said 'don't mess with me today.' She fumbled around looking for her keys in her large leather handbag, and finally yanked them out when she did find them, spilling the contents from her bag onto the cold and dirty concrete in the process. With obvious frustration, Tanya snatched her belongings up, clawing at them with her big glitzy nails, and shoved them back into her bag before climbing into the car and slamming the door. It took her five times before the engine roared into life. It sounded like a faulty starter on her car to me, but she was also clearly angry and agitated, exacerbating the problem and making it even harder than normal to start her vehicle. Her movements were fast and frantic. She screeched out of the parking lot, happy to be escaping her job, and into the flow of the afternoon traffic.

In a rush, she drove to her house, sounding her horn numerous times, even leaning out of the window to give someone the finger and yell at them. And to be fair, the guy did deserve it, cutting her off and nearly pushing her off the road. But it was a far cry from the calm and sympathetic ear I found when she served me at the bar, the pleasant woman who spoke tenderly to me—albeit about my concocted predicament—but then everyone has their breaking point. And on the journey home, Tanya had reached hers.

I called Casey once we were five minutes away from the house, letting her know that Tanya wasn't too far away and to get out of the property before she was discovered there. She responded quickly, and assured me she was on her way out.

As we approached the house, I saw no sign of

Casey. That was good and although it was what I expected, it was still a relief. I had the utmost faith in Casey's ability to get out of there stealthily, but this aspect of the operation was outside of my power, and whenever something was outside my direct control, I felt a degree of concern. It wasn't a worry, as such, more a healthy investment in the success or otherwise of events.

The semi-detached house was just one block from the corner of the main road, and the road's high level of incessant noise was sure to affect anyone's sleep pattern. It would have driven me nuts.

Sleep is such an important factor in well-being. From anger management to weight-loss to decision-making, quality sleep is the great regulator. The ultimate reset button. I once lived close to a busy main road, much like Tanya's house, and I had never been in so many fights in my life. Not just verbal fights but physical altercations. Not that a fist fight was a rarity for me, but when I got into a fight on the way to work, had a fight on the job and then another on the way home, I knew things had gotten out of hand.

Tanya's house was clapboard, and the noise was sure to travel through the thin walls. A lot of trucks used West Fullerton Avenue, especially early in the morning. Maybe she was used to it by now and had become desensitized, but there was nothing I liked less than a consistent lack of sleep caused by excessive noise in the night. There was a good reason why sleep deprivation was considered a form of torture and was effective at breaking a person's will to live.

I drove past the house once, before turning and parking across the other side of the road, under a large oak tree. The street was busy, cars coming and going to the nearby apartment complexes, and people walking to the shops close by.

On the street in front of their home, I saw a car arrive, and out stepped Kyle. Tanya came out the front door to meet him as if she had been watching at the window for his arrival, and it was immediately clear she was not there to simply welcome him home. Tanya and Kyle instantly broke out into an argument. And a heated argument at that. She was throwing her hands in the air and he was trying his best to pacify her. Something had rubbed Tanya the wrong way.

Something was not going well for them.

The question was: what?

I opened my window a crack and strained to hear what the argument was about. They were loud enough for me to hear their voices, but other than the odd word here and there, I couldn't make it out over the other droning background noises in the street. Every time I nearly could hear something a vehicle would rush by and I'd lose it again, leaving me with nothing of practical value to work with.

After five minutes the argument faded out, they

both embraced in a hug and walked inside together.

If Millie was inside, I was sure she would be safe. There was no way I could see Tanya harming her child for any reason whatsoever. She might've had an angry streak, a short fuse that flared up every so often when things became too much but she didn't seem the sort of psychopath that could harm their own child.

But then, that wasn't what Chase was paying me for. He wasn't paying me to assess the safety or otherwise of his daughter, or the mental state and capacity of his former wife.

He was paying me to find Millie, and bring her back before he had to make the drop of a cool million dollars.

Even if Tanya was trying to blackmail Chase, did I see her as the criminal? She was trying to provide a life for Millie, and money could certainly help there, I understood that well enough.

Was I concerned about earning the money Chase offered, taking his money to do the job?

Of course. Without a doubt. Not too many jobs come around with that sort of money. It was a bit of a gold mine. And the price of gold was on the rise.

But would I risk Millie's life to get it?

Not a chance.

Some things are worth more than money, including the life of a child. Especially the life of a child. Her wellbeing. Her happiness. Her security and health.

After five minutes of watching their house, Casey walked beside the truck and got in.

I looked at her expectantly.

"Anything?"

Casey shook her head with a despondent frown.

"Nothing. No sign of Millie, or that she's been there in the last week. There's a lot of kid's tableware in the cupboards, but none of it in the almost full dishwasher. I'd say there was at least three days of dishes in the dishwasher, and not one of them was for a child. No plastic cups, no plastic forks, no plastic bowls. Millie's bedroom was perfectly tidy, the bed was perfectly made and the house was spotless. There were no toys strewn chaotically around like you would expect with a child in the house. Clearly, she's not keeping Millie there."

I thought for a moment.

"If it was Kyle or Tanya at the garage two days ago, then I doubt whether they had a plan B. If their first plan had been disturbed, then Millie would be here."

"And there was no sign of her." Casey nodded in agreement.

"Did you hear their argument?" I asked hopefully.

"Argument?" Casey responded. "When was that?"

"I guess not," I sighed, no such luck.

"Any trouble getting in?"

"Not at all. The backyard was enclosed, and the

backdoor key was under the mat. Lax security if I ever saw it. Not that I'm complaining, it was as easy as they come."

"Didn't leave a trace that you were there, did you?"

Casey gave me a look that would wither a dragon. I put my hands up in mock surrender.

"Ok, ok, of course not. Forget I asked. Anything else?"

"Not really. I took some photos." Casey pulled out her phone and passed it across to me. "A few unpaid utility bills lying around, a large power bill, and five phone bills. Could explain the need for a quick hit of cash, but nothing to suggest they've done anything about it. Everything seems very, very normal. Not a sign that anything is wrong or a break from the ordinary."

I punched the steering wheel lightly. That wasn't what I needed to hear.

I needed a clue, something to work off, something to build this case upon. Anything, no matter how small to get things moving and create momentum. At the moment, that all important factor seemed to have ceased.

"Do you think if Chase found out that it was Tanya, that he would press charges against her for blackmail?" Casey asked as she started sending the photos over to my phone.

"Without a doubt he would."

"Even if it wouldn't be in the best interests for Millie?"

I gripped the steering wheel tightly, squeezing hard into its solid and unyielding rubber until my knuckles turned white.

"Chase Martin is a prick. A prick of the highest order. He doesn't care about Tanya one bit, and he doesn't care about Kyle either, that's for sure. He cares more about his precious money than getting his little girl back safe and well. Which stinks. He seemed more concerned with losing a million dollars. That's his big worry in this whole sordid business, the bottom line. Imagine that, what a low life. There are only two true loves in Chase Martin's life—money and himself, of course, the narcissistic slimeball. I don't think Millie really matters, not in the way a young child does for a normal well-adjusted parent. But then Chase Martin is clearly not a well-adjusted person. I'm not saying Millie isn't important to him, just that she's important only up to a point, and not beyond, a bit like his favorite car—he's fond of it, he's even proud of it, but he's never going to put it first in his life, and Millie's the same."

"Why do we even do this?" Casey shook her head, her hair falling across her face.

"Because it's our job. We investigate. It's what we know and it's what we do."

Casey looked out the window wistfully. "Sometimes I wish I was an office worker, just showing up nine-to-five, Monday to Friday."

I gave a little laugh. "No, you don't. And you know it. You'd hate it, even more than you're hating this right now."

Casey laughed too. "You're right. I wouldn't last a week."

"A week! You wouldn't even last a day. And nor would I." I turned to Casey, serious again. "This is our job. And as much as we don't like Chase, we're going to see this through to the bitter end. No matter where it leads and what the outcome is."

I started the truck and began the drive to drop Casey off at her apartment.

I had someplace to go tonight, someplace that couldn't wait any longer.

CHAPTER 17

HUGH GUTHRIE was where I thought he would be—celebrating his win in his favorite restaurant.

The atmosphere was jovial as I walked into the Italian eatery. There was a bar to one side of the room, and twenty-five or so tables to the other side. The tables were covered with red and white patterned cloths, the chairs looked like they were bought in the seventies, and the upper walls were filled with photos of the owner and various famous customers.

I sat at the bar, ordered a bourbon, and watched Guthrie from a distance.

He was laughing, cheering. A smile as wide as the Cheshire cat.

Someone was dead, killed with his hands, and he was laughing because the law couldn't put him behind bars. That was when the system failed. How could a technicality let a killer walk free? How could a mistake in evidence allow a murderer to walk the streets again? That I would never understand.

Hugh Guthrie killed fellow newscaster Brian Gates, and now he was celebrating with joy. That made the grip on my glass tighter.

But worse than that, he gave the gun to the boy that shot up Claire's school. Out of a need to be front and center in the news, he handed the gun to a mentally unstable teenager, pushing the boy to make the story. Guthrie had been following the teen, documenting his life, hoping for a story that would win him the Pulitzer Prize for journalism.

When the story didn't materialize, Guthrie pushed the kid in the direction that the story desperately needed—a school shooting. Amongst the many people that the boy killed was my Claire, as she was desperately sheltering the young children in her class from the barrage of bullets.

The kid, Alexander Logan, died the day of the shooting, robbing me of any sense of justice.

The man who gave Alexander the gun had to be held responsible. Without Guthrie's push, without Guthrie's encouragement, the school shooting would never have happened. That was hard to prove, and even harder to get a conviction, but it was the truth.

And I thought Guthrie was going to pay. I thought the justice system was going to sentence him to life in prison for the murder of Brian Gates.

But the law let me down.

Guthrie looked up from his celebration and caught me staring at him.

I didn't flinch, holding my stare.

The smile disappeared from his face, and for a few moments, he turned back to his friends, before excusing himself. I'd done work for Guthrie years before, and later, I convinced him to confess to the murder of Brian Gates. Most people are convinced to tell the truth after I slam my car into theirs and hold a gun to their head.

Guthrie didn't confront me inside. I didn't expect him to. Guthrie was in his fifties, weak, and sly. He looked at me, and stepped out the front doors of the restaurant. He didn't want to cause a scene in front of his friends, I understood that, especially today, but it was risky for him to walk out onto the street with me.

I knocked back the rest of my bourbon, threw a few notes on the bar, and walked out the doors, following Guthrie onto the street.

"I'm packing." He held open his jacket for me to see his holster and weapon as soon as I stepped outside. "I thought you'd track me down; however, I didn't think it would be this quickly. Not when I was celebrating."

The sidewalk was quiet, as was the street, and no witnesses would've seen us.

I could've taken him out right there and then, and I would've enjoyed it, but then I would be arrested within the hour. I couldn't afford that risk right now. Not when Millie's life was still on the line.

Now wasn't the time to get physical.

"You think your little revolver would stop me?" I stepped close, towering over him. "You wouldn't be able to draw that thing quick enough to stop me."

Guthrie stepped back, bumping into the brick wall behind him. "What do you want, Valentine? I beat the law. The courts said I was innocent. The—"

"The courts didn't say you were innocent." I snarled, bringing my nose close to his. "They said that they didn't have enough evidence to convict you. That doesn't mean you're innocent. You're a killer. A cold-blooded murderer. And I'm going to make sure that you get what's coming."

"You couldn't," he scoffed. "You can't stop me."

"I'm your karma, Hugh." I pressed my finger into his chest. "Get a good look at my face, because I'm the person that will see that you go down. I don't care which crime they get you for, but I will make sure that the memory of my wife will get justice."

He tried to move back further, but he was squashed against the wall.

"You don't want to make enemies with me, Valentine." He tried to sound tough, but I could smell the fear rolling off him. "I know how to play the system. I know how to play the game. And if you threaten me, then I will strike first. Consider this a warning."

"You're going to threaten me?" I grabbed his collar and pressed my fist into his throat. "I will make sure that you pay for your involvement in the school shooting, Guthrie. Mark my words."

"Everything ok here?"

We turned. It was two beat cops. They were

walking their route, wondering if they should get involved. One cop had his hand on his weapon, the other was cautious but open.

"Everything is fine, officer." I let go of Guthrie's collar. "Isn't it, Hugh?"

Hugh looked at me, and then to the cops. The fear in his eyes was clear, but he played the game. All he wanted to do was go back inside to his friends and celebrate the fact that he beat the system.

"Everything is fine." Guthrie patted himself down, and straightened his collar. "We're just some old friends talking."

The cops watched as Guthrie stood next to me.

"It's good to see you, Valentine." He patted me on the arm. "But attack is always the best form of defense. And you've just made yourself a very powerful enemy."

I watched Guthrie walk back into the restaurant, no doubt to laugh and drink and celebrate, and then I turned to the officers, who were still waiting for me to move.

I grunted, before walking down the street, away from the scene. I couldn't afford trouble tonight.

But I was sure that trouble was going to follow me in the future.

And it would have Hugh Guthrie's name written all over it.

CHAPTER 18

CHASE MARTIN was waiting at my office when I returned. He was waiting by the door, phone in hand, hair a mess. He looked uncharacteristically disheveled, if 'disheveled' was ever a word to describe someone still wearing the very best designer clothes that money could buy. But there was a world-weary look about him from the stress and pressure. His posture was slumped and he looked worn down and fatigued. His normal smug arrogance was currently absent. I wondered how long it would last. It was a look that I had not yet witnessed on Chase. But then he needed taking down a few pegs so I can't say I particularly felt sorry for him in this moment. For Millie, yes, always, but not Chase. He had caused enough hurt, pain and misery in his time to warrant more than a fair share himself, and he was now finally getting a taste of it too. And by the looks of it he didn't like it. Not one bit. Something had clearly got to him. And I was curious to find out what.

"Tell me you've found her, Jack." There was stress in his voice, almost a desperate panic. "Tell me that you've found my Millie."

"Let's talk about that inside."

I opened my office door with the key, swinging the door wide open.

My office was in a good location, in the Loop, amid the hustle and bustle of good old Downtown Chicago, the beating heart of the city. Its very essence. There was no signage on the street, no listing in the building directory, nor, heaven forbid the yellow pages, and only my name on a small nondescript plaque on the door. If you didn't know it was there, you'd never see it. My office was on the second floor, and strategically so, mostly to prevent any curious walk-ins off the street. You know, the sort of people who weren't really looking for a private investigator, but on seeing a sign for one decide to come in and waste time with stupid questions about following their partner, husband or wife, whom they suspect of having an affair. That sort of work might be the mainstay of your average yellow pages P.I. but it sure wasn't mine, nor was it the type of business that I wanted or would ever accept. That sort of thing was amateur hour, anyone could do it with a half decent camera and a video recorder. The cases I took had a bit of punch to them, which was the way I liked it.

People came looking for me. That's the type of work I needed. Those desperate for assistance who could really utilize my skill set, which when you've been in the game as long as I had, was extensive. And if they really needed to find me, and they persevered in doing so, then they'd manage it, sure enough.

Inside my office door was the foyer office, filled by a long desk with two computer monitors, usually where Casey sat. It was the most organized and tidy section of our workspace. Not that to an outsider's eye it really appeared that way, until they saw the bombsite of my own little corner of the office. There was a worn old couch next to the door, and a potted plant next to that in a constant state of dehydration from lack of consistent watering. The poor thing was in a permanent state of barely clinging onto life as a result. I should have chucked it in the trash but I sort of admired its tenacity and so would drown it in water to try and bring it back from the brink, only to forget about it again until it looked like it was once more about to give up the ghost.

I had the pleasure of traveling to Ireland a number of times, a stunning place with hilarious people, who explained to me how much a 'pot plant' livens up the office. I instantly assumed that they meant a marijuana plant—and I'm sure that would liven up any office. It wasn't until a week later, when an elderly lady talked about her 'pot plants' at home that I realized that pot plants were the same as potted plants here.

To the side of the room was a white board, filled with my incoherent scribbles, and a number of post-it notes. Trying to plot out the links between suspects, evidence and the victim, seeking to order these into some sort of coherent logical way that ultimately would identify the perpetrator. Not that I was succeeding so far with this case. Things were foggy to say the least.

To the back of the room was another door, the one to my separate office.

I led Chase into my office and offered him a whiskey.

I could see he thought I worked in a pigsty. It was written all over his face. But I didn't care what he thought. Or anyone else for that matter. They could take me as they found me or get the hell out.

"How can you drink at a time like this?" His hand went to his forehead.

"What's changed?" I questioned as I dropped a cube of ice into the glass, slowly rotating it in my palm so the liquid spiraled in the glass, releasing its malty aroma. "You seem more frantic."

He paused, and almost fell down into the chair opposite my desk. "I took the money out of the bank. All of it. My hard-earned money. I worked so hard for that money, and I deserve to keep it."

I felt my jaw harden, and my fingers tightened around the glass.

"Right. The money," I muttered through gritted teeth. "Of course."

I moved around my desk and slowly placed my drink down on the table, before sitting down.

"It's in the safe in my penthouse. One million dollars in cold, hard cash. It's a lot of money, Valentine, an awful lot of money, and I don't want to lose it to some criminals. They don't deserve my money. Nobody does but me. It's mine."

I bit my tongue as the dialogue in my head explained to him that I thought he was the criminal— a fraudster, a corrupt piece of dirt, if I ever met one. That he was the man who I should be after and put away behind bars. And that the world would be a far better place as a result.

Chase stood and moved to the door. He was clearly struggling to stay still. He held his arms across his chest, staring at the ground.

"I didn't talk to Ruby, but her father returned home and said that she'd gone to L.A. He flew there with her. I don't know if I believe him," Chase said. "Maybe now is the time to call the cops? I don't want to lose the money."

"What about Millie?"

"Millie will be fine." He was almost dismissive.

"And if she's not?"

He shook his head, and then began pacing the room, agitated and jumpy, trying to use up all his nervous energy, which was almost spilling out of him.

"She has to be. I couldn't live with myself," he whispered.

At last, a glimpse of humanity.

He paced the floor a while longer, before he

turned back to me.

"Do you think I should call the cops? I've never had a good experience with them. They hate me. I've got enemies there. People who would love nothing more than to lock me up."

"It wouldn't be the cops. The FBI would handle this case, and maybe you're right. Maybe it's time to hand it over to an organization with unlimited resources and manpower." I leaned forward on the table. "We've investigated all the major suspects, and we haven't come up with much. We've felt like we've got close, but in the end, we've got nothing concrete. The drop is in two days. Just two days, Chase. If you're going to call them, now is the time to do so."

"No, no." He shook his hand at me. "Not the FBI. I can't have them snooping around my business. I'm already on their radar and this would be the perfect reason for them to get into my files. They would turn my penthouse upside down before they had even considered Millie. They wouldn't care about her."

"What do they want you for?" I quizzed, doing my best to sound surprised.

He looked shocked that he had just given that information away.

"Nothing." He shook his head hard. "It's nothing. A disgruntled investor reported me, but they had nothing solid. The lead of the case, Special Agent Ramon Wright, said he was going to make sure that I would go down and then started stalking me, day and night. For a month, every time I left my apartment, he was there with a smug look on his face. He dragged me into an interview, but I lawyered up, and didn't say much. I told him that I'd done nothing illegal, but he was adamant that he was going to get me. Hasn't managed it yet though and I'll be damned if I'll be the architect of my own downfall by inviting him in."

I sipped my whiskey.

"But," A thought went through Chase's mind. "Do you think that the FBI set this up? As an excuse so that they could search my apartment? Of course, they would have. They've wanted to search my apartment for a year, and I won't let them. No judge will sign off on a search warrant of my place with the small amount of evidence that they have. And it's all circumstantial anyway. But if I invited them to talk about the kidnapping? Then they could take their liberty. They'd go through everything with a fine-tooth comb, going through my private business, my accounts, my files, stuff that has nothing to do with them. Maybe it's all just one big set up."

"I doubt that's the case," I responded. "But that's not entirely impossible."

"I can't have them involved." He sighed. "And that's just my luck—when you need them, you can't go to them. And when you don't need them, they're on you like a swarm of bees."

Chase paced the floor again.

"There aren't many crimes that happen over a long

period of time," I said. "That's why kidnappings are so hard. You know that the crime is taking place, you know that something is happening, but you don't know where to go. We've all heard the stories of ransoms being paid, and the kidnapped victim still turning up dead. There's a lot at risk here."

Chase nodded. "One million dollars is a lot of cash."

"I was talking about Millie."

"Of course." He quickly agreed. "What's our next step?"

I took another sip of whiskey. After Chase left my office, I was going to need another one. Just being in the presence of this man makes me angry. He had an unusual presence about him, a sort of stench, not of the body but of character. There was just something repellent about Chase, that although difficult to define was easy enough to recognize, which made me sick whenever I was near him.

"We've looked at all major suspects, and we've got nothing. We've looked into all the people that you've suggested could be involved, and we have no further leads. It's time to take this to the next level. It's time to prepare for the end of this."

"Meaning?"

"Meaning that it's time to prepare for the drop and prepare to save Millie's life."

CHAPTER 19

THE PLAYGROUND looked so different on a weekday. More stay-at-home Moms and less Dads making up for lost time. There were a handful of nannies too, they were more interested in good gossip, on catching up and swapping notes than whether little Jenny could finally manage the monkey bars yet, or if Johnny could ride his beloved bike without his training wheels. And the kids didn't need their approval, they were happier just to play today outside in the clear fresh air. It was calmer, more relaxed. The atmosphere was still jovial, the laughter of children sliding down the play equipment was joyous and infectious. There were happy smiles, beaming eyes, and little running legs. I could sit next to the playground all day and listen to the happy children laughing. But I wouldn't do that. That would be creepy. Or at least perceived as such. In a way that made me sad, that something pure and beautiful had been tarnished by a small minority of twisted weirdoes.

I couldn't help but think of Claire at times like this. Of what we could have had together before it was so cruelly taken away. Of the son or daughter we could have raised and loved, and watched grow and thrive. I think I would have made a good parent. Claire definitely would, no doubt about it, she was always so patient, so soft and caring, with a real nurturing heart. You could almost say she was made for motherhood. It would have been a world of bliss for us both. That all seemed so distant now. Almost like a dream. My life had changed incomparably since her murder. There was an emptiness in my heart that I had now come to terms with, accepting that it would always be my bedfellow. Still, despite my stress, despite my anger, despite my lack of sleep right now, I found it hard not to smile today. The children were all so happy, so free and so innocent.

And yet, these parents didn't know that a child had been taken from this very spot only three days ago. Three days down, two days to go. Time was ticking. The top of the hourglass was less than half full now, and the sand always seemed to move faster the closer to empty it became. Rushing frantically in the final moments. And then finally it's all used up and gone forever.

I was starting to feel the pressure, and with pressure comes doubt. I was beginning to question my instincts. I had to go over all the possibilities again to sharpen my focus. Why had I been so quick to dismiss professional kidnappers? If it was a professional group of kidnappers, then these parents deserved to know, they deserved to understand the threat. Any of their children could be the next victim, their child snatched and held who knows where, while a demand for a cool million dollars was levied at their door.

My instincts told me that was not the threat. Why?

It was too open, with too many witnesses. Millie had been too easy to lure away, she hadn't caused a fuss, there were no reports of a scream, a struggle, of anything. It was so much more likely that it was someone she knew. Someone she trusted and would go with freely, even happily. Maybe someone she loved. Maybe even someone that loved her.

And five days was a long time to hold a child you didn't know. Professionals needed it over in twenty-four hours, forty-eight at the most. The longer they had the kid, the more chance they had of getting caught. It upped the stakes for all involved and that wasn't what the kidnappers needed. They needed to minimize the risk and they needed the money as quickly as possible, with as little fuss as possible. And then they needed to disappear without a trace forever.

It had to be someone that Chase knew or was associated with, someone who wanted to take his money. And that's what this was about—money. That cold, harsh greenery. The lottery offered worse odds to make someone a millionaire, but it also didn't come with the threat of life in prison if you got it wrong.

No risk, no reward.

But then maybe it wasn't just about gaining money. Maybe that was part of it but not the whole story. Perhaps to whoever was responsible it was just as important to take it away from Chase. To see him humbled. Brought to his knees. For Chase to know what it was to be fleeced, like he'd done to so many others before. Maybe that was the overriding motivating factor, to give Chase an almighty dose of his own medicine and teach him a lesson he would never forget.

I scanned the park again, taking in every detail.

Not only was it the place of the kidnapping, it was also the drop-zone for the money, which suggested that the kidnapper knew this place well. Even intimately. It made sense. You'd want to know all the entry and exit points, all the potential hazards and danger zones. It must have been a place that was very familiar to the kidnapper, somewhere they came often and possibly still did, following their normal routine so as not to arouse any suspicion. It was an interesting thought: that the kidnapper might have been back here over the last few days. Who maybe was even here right now. Or who maybe was watching the area and us.

But there was no way to know one way or the other.

There were no surveillance cameras pointed at the park, the shops all had closing times around 5pm, and the streets surrounding the park would be quiet at midnight. The set-up for the drop was perfect.

I studied the street map closely—there were only two real escape routes the kidnapper could take. One led them straight to the express way, where it would be easy to escape out of the city, and the other led them further into the suburbs, where it would be easy to lose a tail amongst the maze of different streets.

Assuming the kidnapper was well organized, I imagined they would have a secondary car close by to switch into, so there wasn't much use looking for license plate numbers. And they would probably use a stolen vehicle anyway. That's what I would have done.

I stared at the large oak tree nearby, a perfect spot to place a small camera. I formulated a plan to return later that night to place a camera in the tree in preparation for the following night. No matter what went down, I needed it recorded. But I had to be careful. For all I knew the kidnapper was watching the area. Maybe watching me right now, and so when I placed the camera it had to be done completely unobserved. Nightfall would be my friend. I'd slip in, climb the tree and place the camera, then slip out again before anyone knew I'd been there.

"There's nothing unusual," Casey commented as she sat next to me on the park bench. "Except for the big guy in the dark glasses sitting on the park bench staring at the children in the playground."

"Funny," I said as I ignored her reference to me. "I couldn't find anything unusual about the shops. None of the store owners have a history of criminal activity. From what I could find they're all Mom and Pop type owners, people who have operated those stores for years and are part of the fabric of the place. Trustworthy members of the local community."

"Who's your front-runner at the moment?"

I stood and Casey followed me as we walked to the edge of the grassed area, next to the under-used dog park.

"Kyle." Just as that thought went through my mind, five loudly barking dogs came up next to us, and a grumpy woman opened the gate. I say grumpy, but death-warmed-over would be a better description.

Her dogs were disheveled, underweight, and loud. They were desperate to let off excess steam, let off stress by running in the park. And living with her appeared to be very stressful.

The woman forcibly opened the yard gate, slammed it shut behind her, and then lit up a cigarette. She took one long, deep drag, letting go of the dogs' leashes, finally giving them a chance to be free.

I stared at her for a moment, the dogs yapping loudly as they fought each other.

"I didn't realize this little patch was a dog park." Casey leaned in close to me. "Not much of a dog park either. It's only a tiny little square. Still, better than

157

nothing, I guess."

"Nobody has been in there in the times we've come here. And I can understand why." I watched as the woman finished her cigarette, and then casually flicked it into the bushes. I couldn't stand people who threw trash all around the place, and it annoyed me immediately. She then went and sat on the bench and opened her phone, no doubt posting about her position in the dog park on social media to appear like she was doing a great thing for her animals. Then one of her dogs took a dump in the dog park. She looked up from her phone and clearly saw but made no effort to bag it up. If I disliked her before, I detested her now. I'm a dog owner and I love my mutt, but without fail I always clean up after him. It's the decent thing to do and she clearly had no decency or class.

"So, you really think it's Kyle?" Casey led us away from the dog park to the street. "I thought you said he was the symbol of decent All-American goodness."

"He's got to be the number one candidate at the moment, which is a concern. I want the number one guy at the moment to be the person who I also believe did it, but I'm not so sure I do. He's a nice guy who has worked extremely hard for his money. If he lost a hundred thousand in an investment, I can guarantee that's his life savings. He would've had plans for that money. Plans for the future. Losing that money was sure to hurt him, and possibly hurt him enough to take revenge."

"And Tanya would've told Kyle not to beat him into the ground because he's Millie's father."

"Exactly. That anger had to come out somehow."

"It could be a 'Murder on the Orient Express' type of situation. You know, where everyone is involved. Maybe Kyle, Tanya, Damon, Ben, and everyone else on that list of people who had lost money are involved. They all could be working together to pull this off. Maybe their joint hatred for Chase has brought them together?"

"Could be. But then the more people who are involved, the more likely it is that one of them will slip up. And no one has so far. We also know that Ruby isn't going to be here for the drop, she's been posting pictures of herself in L.A. There is no way she would've taken Millie with her."

"True, but she could've still set it up from the start."

I pondered that thought as we walked across the road, stopping on the sidewalk to look back at the park. The location where the crime had occurred just three days before. I tried to picture the scene in my mind's eye as it would have unfolded, searching it for clues, for information, for something new and previously overlooked that I could work with.

"Guessing is about all we can do now. Our best chance of securing the girl, and keeping the money, is getting the drop right. I'm coming back at midnight to set the place up—small cameras and the works." I shook my head as the woman from the dog park started screaming at her dogs. "But we're going to have to ride this one out."

"The risk is going to be high."

"We're not going to risk Millie. No matter what Chase wants us to do with the money, we're not going to risk the life of that precious little girl for his cash."

CHAPTER 20

MY FAVORITE bar was the perfect escape.

Dark, somber, and separate from the rest of the world. It was a little haven where I felt centered and could think. Filled with people who needed to escape, people who needed to disappear for a while, just like me. After three pints of Goose Island IPA, I finally raised my eyes from the glass in front of me, and looked to the television. There was a game on. The Cubs were playing, and that elicited the occasional noise from the people around the bar. Every now and again, I joined in on the collective groans. And groans it was. The Cubs hadn't been having the best season, and the locals were beginning to feel it.

The bar was filled tonight, not for any special occasion except escapism. But that's as good a reason as any in my book. There was a group that I didn't know—not locals, could be bikers, could be gang members. We had that sometimes, travelers drifting through the area, looking for the right place to pick a fight, and they were directed here by some unknowing local. The fights that happened in our bar didn't last long—although I couldn't name the people next to me, although I had no idea what these people did with their lives outside this bar, they were my family. A family of misfits, lost loners, but a family no less. If one of us was to throw a fist, we all would join in.

I tried to watch the game, tried to bring myself into the intensity of the innings, but I couldn't switch off the thoughts running wild in my head. The batter swung hard, throwing his entire bodyweight behind the hit. The people around me made comments about his possible steroid use, how he had bulked up massively since last season and that he had missed a drug test, but I just couldn't bring myself into the game nor the gossip.

The thoughts of Millie had taken over everything.

It was no longer a case, it was no longer a job, it was a determined mission to save a girl's life. One that I couldn't bear to let anything happen to.

My mind was racing through the possibilities, but with three pints in me and less than thirty hours to go until the drop, the adrenaline coursing through my veins wouldn't let my mind settle on anything long enough to figure out what was what. I was running on empty. Fueled now by nervous energy and fear. I didn't mind admitting it, but I was scared. Scared something would happen to that young girl, something that I could never forgive myself for. There was no shortage of guilt already in my life and I didn't need the death of Millie added to it. I guess that was selfish, in a sense. Although Millie's wellbeing was my main concern, I was worried about my own sanity too if things went wrong. And it's not like they'd exactly gone right so far anyway.

Mentally, I flicked from one potential perpetrator to the next. Kyle. Tanya. Ruby. Damon. Ben.

Every so often, Claire's face floated into my mind and I shook my head hard to displace it. I couldn't let my love for her affect my judgment. I needed to think clearly, to focus on the problem at hand.

Maybe it was too late for that. The doubts were coming back. Now thick and fast. I'd been through every scenario, checked out every suspect and what had I come up with? Nothing. Nothing of substance anyway. If ever there was a case I needed closed, and for the right reasons, it was this one. I needed to find Millie, to know that she was safe and well, and that she was back with her loving mother. At the moment I knew none of those things. For all I knew she could be dead. Or worse. I shuddered at the thought. It didn't bear thinking about. However, I couldn't ignore it either.

Maybe it was time to call the FBI, to utilize their unrivaled resources and manpower, even if it was against Chase's wishes. The person who had hired me in the first place. I was good at what I did, I knew that, but at the end of the day I was just one man, albeit one man working with one hell of an assistant. Still, Casey and I didn't compare to the investigative juggernaut that the feds were, for all their failings.

I didn't care about what Chase was hiding in that apartment, whether it was money, or files, or plans to rip people off. That wasn't my concern. I only cared about getting that little girl back safely. If the FBI needed to nail Chase for ripping some people off, then so be it.

But I wouldn't contact them.

I couldn't.

There was too much risk. Another kidnapping in Florida had gone wrong with the FBI's involvement. That didn't look good, and it didn't look promising. I couldn't have a dead girl on my conscience.

What could they do anyway? I'd already looked at every lead, and they all led nowhere. They would show up, take over the case, and likely botch another money-drop. They didn't have the delicate touch. They'd lose the money and the girl trying to follow their procedures. It wasn't a risk I was willing to take. I had to find her myself.

"Hit it!" I shouted aggressively at the screen, my hand gripped tight around my glass. "Take a swing! Damn it!"

The people around me sat back, stunned by my sudden show of aggression. Usually, I was the calm one, the one that nicely brought other people back into line. They weren't used to seeing me like this. I was agitated. Frustrated and angry.

"Cubs don't have a chance." The call came from

one of the blow-ins on the other side of the bar. One of the guys dressed in black jeans, black t-shirt and leather jacket. Long black hair, tattoos running up his neck. He was shorter than me, maybe 5'10, but he weighed more than me. If he wasn't looking so angry, I might've rubbed his belly for good luck. "Cubs are hopeless this year."

"You're a brave man walking into this bar and saying that."

"Yeah?" The man slid off his bar stool and walked over to me. "Why would that be?"

Usually, I would've landed a left hook there and then. It was my favorite punch: closer to the target than the right hand when in an orthodox boxing stance, but a real power shot. I would've lined him up, asked him a question, whether real or frivolous, it didn't matter, and then in that split second while his mind was processing the question and his response, I would have swung hard before he was ready. After all, it's the punches you don't see or expect that have the greatest effect. And then when he was sprawled on the ground, I would have turned to the bar tender and handed the situation over to him. He would have told the rest of them to drag him out of here, shot gun in his hand. And it wouldn't have been the first time.

But I couldn't risk an energy sapping fight. I still had a job to do.

I still had to go to the park and watch for the kidnapper at midnight, and if there was no sign of them, I had to plant the cameras in preparation for the next night. And I had to do this carefully with an attention to detail. I had to keep my mind on the job and my head in the game.

"I don't know where you've blown in from, but in Chicago, we talk nicely to strangers."

That made him smile. He was already missing a few teeth, and I would've happily knocked some more out, but turned back to the television.

"I'm not from around here, but I'll happily drive you to the hospital after I beat you into the dirt."

That pushed my buttons.

"Not in here." The bartender could see my hand grip around the glass tighter. "Not tonight, boys. Not here. You." He pointed to the guy picking the fight. "Go back to your friends and finish your drink, and then get out of here. This isn't the place to be picking fights."

The guy didn't move.

"Did you hear me?" The bartender shouted. Everyone in the bar turned around.

The situation was on knife-edge.

I stood, towering over the man.

"Oi!" It was the bartender again. He was reaching for something. The shotgun, I would imagine. "I said, settle it down!"

The guy didn't move and nor did I.

Luckily, one of his friends came between us, and pushed him back. They walked back to the pool table at the end of the bar, knocking back their drinks.

I sat back down and indicated I needed another drink.

"Not tonight, Jack." The bartender said. "I could see it in your eyes the second you walked in here. You're looking for a fight. You're looking for someone to take the blame for whatever situation you've got yourself in to. I like you, Jack, but I don't need any trouble in here. You're cut-off tonight. Best if you take off now. Understand?"

I stared at him for a moment, part of me still wanted to make an issue out of it, but he was right.

I nodded and stood to leave.

"Not that way, pal. Not out the front." It was the bartender again. "10 to 1 your buddy will be out there waiting for you, along with his buddies. I don't need you two getting back into it, blocking my doorway with your fighting, interrupting everyone's evening with a visit from the law. I'll show you out the back."

As I followed him down the dark staff corridor, my mind was getting back to work. I still had five hours until midnight, and that left me with time to kill, and anger to burn.

It was time to take a chance.

CHAPTER 21

WITH A few pints under my belt, my decision-making process wasn't the best.

My decision making was never that good, but under the influence of beer, it was even worse than normal. I was too impulsive with drink in me. I didn't think things through. And I took needless risks. But then, sometimes, that's what's needed. Sometimes who dares does win and you need to say 'what the hell' and throw it all into 'who gives a damn gear' and then wait to see where the chips fall.

Outside of the bar, I climbed on board my truck and decided it was time to take a chance. I fired up the engine, revved it twice until it screamed for mercy, as if a mirror to my mood, and hit the gas, screeching the tires out of the gravel parking lot, and hitting the highway. I was driving like a man possessed, weaving in and out of the late-night traffic, propelled forward by my determination and my resolution to see through the drastic action that I had in mind.

I had a goal and nothing was going to stop me.

I had to save that girl.

The longer it took to get to my destination, the

more the rage inside me bubbled. Building and building until I felt ready to explode. When I pulled up to the sidewalk outside Tanya's front door, I was fully wired, like a prize bull ready to burst out of the gates at a rodeo. I didn't have time to formulate a coherent plan. This wasn't the time to stop and think. But I knew the basics of what I was going to do and, more importantly, what I needed to achieve.

I stormed out of my truck, slamming the door behind me, ran up to the front door of the Logan Square home, and banged on it hard with my fist. Waiting for a response, I looked around the street. No witnesses. Good. That was just the way I liked it.

Kyle answered the door. That was also good.

He opened it wide, standing in the doorway proudly. He was a step above me, but that leveled out our difference in height. Kyle even had a smile on his face as he said 'hello,' a warm welcome to his home. But this was no time for pleasantries.

That smile was quickly wiped away as I flung my fist into his throat. I gripped hard on his windpipe, squeezing the fragile tissue there into a contorted mass inside my knuckle white fist. He wheezed violently, the air departing from his lungs, as his eyes widened in shock and fear. He fell backwards like a sack of potatoes. I stepped inside, my handgun drawn from my belt, and I pointed it into his face. Kicking his legs out of the way, I pushed the front door shut behind me. I was inside and concealed.

Tanya stepped out of the kitchen, drying her hands on a towel, to see what the commotion was all about. The color drained from her face and she froze when she saw I had the gun to Kyle's face.

"You." I grunted to Tanya. "On the floor, face down. Hands on the back of your head."

She whimpered quietly but did as she was told. Kyle struggled to breathe, grabbing frantically at his throat. I gave him a final aggressive squeeze then let him go with a push, shoving his skull into the carpeted floor.

The hallway was wide but dimly lit. A rug ran up the middle of the walkway, stained with a couple of muddy footprints.

"Whatever you need, just take it," Tanya said with her face squashed in the carpet. "I have jewelry upstairs, but that's about all I have. My purse is in the kitchen. Whatever you need, just take it and leave us alone. We don't have a lot. Please don't harm us. Please don't kill us. I beg you."

I ignored her and kept my focus on Kyle. He was breathing more easily but now had beads of sweat appearing on his forehead and I could tell he wasn't entirely surprised to see me.

"You know what I need." I snarled at Kyle. "You know why I've come here."

Kyle looked to Tanya first, face down on the floor, and then back to me. "It's not here. Not yet."

"Where is it?"

"I'm getting it, ok?" He responded, relaxing a little and rubbing his throat. "I just need another two days and I'll have it all. Just two more days. I promise."

"You don't have two days. You've got exactly five minutes before I pull this trigger."

"What's he talking about?" Tanya questioned, face down. "Kyle?"

"Not now, Tanya." Kyle didn't take his eyes off the gun this time.

"Kyle, what's he talking about!" Tanya raised her head.

"Not now!" he responded.

"Kyle! What sort of trouble are you in?!" Tanya's voice was starting to crack, whether from fear or anger, I couldn't quite tell.

"Yeah, Kyle." I grunted. "What sort of trouble are you in? Why don't you tell this good woman what sort of trouble you're in?"

"I'll get it." He pleaded to me. "I promise. Just two days and I'll have the money."

"The money?" I questioned. "What money?"

"All of it. The whole five grand. A guy told me that he can get my money back in two days. I'll have more than enough to pay you back then. I promise. I'll have it in cash."

"What five grand?" I leaned forward. "You think I'm here for money?"

A look of complete confusion washed over his face. "What?"

"What are you talking about, Kyle?" I leaned in closer, gun still in my hand, pointed at his head.

"The money that I was lent to pay the lawyer. The five grand. I've got it. I just need two more days to pay it back. I know I said I'd have it last month, but things were tight. I'll have it next week. I promise."

I lowered my gun, just a touch.

"And what did you need a lawyer for, Kyle?"

"What do you care?" Kyle looked over at Tanya, a pleading look in his eyes. "I'm sorry, honey. I know you didn't want me using a loan shark again, but the lawyer was so sure he would get the money back, then I could pay back the loan and we'd be on easy street. The lawyer guaranteed me that he could build a case against him. He was sure that there was enough evidence to take it to court. And it's not just for us, but for all the guys that were conned."

Tanya looked ready to explode, gun or no gun. "First you pawn the only thing of value we own and now you've brought debt collectors to our door." She looked ready to jump up and knock him out herself. "What if Millie had been at home? How dare you put her in danger!"

I stepped between them and gestured for her to lie back down on the floor. This was my show.

"If it wasn't for your dirt bag ex-husband," Kyle grunted. "I wouldn't have needed to do it."

I interrupted Kyle by waving the gun in his face. "Tell me why you needed a lawyer."

He glared at me for a moment.

"I needed a lawyer to try and sue her ex, a guy named Chase Martin, for losing our money. He ripped us off. It was all a great big con and the lawyer said he could prove it in court."

"You tried to sue Chase?" Tanya raised her head again, but kept her stomach on the ground. "And you didn't tell me?!"

"Don't move." I pointed the gun at her. "Keep talking, Kyle. How are you getting the money back to pay for the lawyer?"

"A guy called me. I don't know who it was. It was an unknown number, and a guy using one of those voice changers. He didn't talk for long, but he said he would get my hundred thousand dollars back from Chase in two more days. I can pay you then. I can even pay interest."

"How was he getting the money back?"

"He didn't say. He just said that he would transfer it to my bank account on Saturday morning."

The thoughts crashed through my head.

"You'd better have the money by then." I tried to cover my tracks. I didn't need them to know that Millie was missing. That would only complicate things further.

"What?" Kyle was confused. "I thought you didn't know about the money? And wait, I know you. You're the guy from the truck stop. From the gym there. What the…?"

"It's not just money, Kyle. It's never just money. I'm keeping tabs on you." I waved the gun in the air. "You've got until Monday to pay the money, or you'll lose everything. More than you can possibly imagine."

He didn't look convinced by my attempt to cover my tracks. In truth, neither was I.

It had to be the kidnapper that contacted Kyle. That's the only way the money would've been deposited back, which meant that the kidnapper wasn't motivated by greed, nor money. This wasn't a kidnapping gang; this wasn't a random attack. This was the work of someone on that list of names.

I had a lead but time was running out to chase it.

"Look after him." Turning to look at Tanya, I waved the gun in Kyle's direction. A look of recognition also washed over her face. "Make sure he sees it through, or there'll be trouble."

CHAPTER 22

FOUR HOURS until midnight, and the adrenaline from my encounter with Kyle and Tanya was still pumping through my veins as I drove my truck back to my house. My vision was focused, my mind was clear, and my heart was still pounding. My plan was to get inside, try and calm myself down with another beer, and then stake out the park around 11pm, before putting up the cameras at 1am. I needed a full stomach for the night ahead, and I had half a left-over pizza in the fridge. Perfect to get me through the night.

My greatest fear was how Chase was going to handle the drop. He might've been good at fooling people in business and sales, but he wasn't prepared for this type of situation in real life. He hadn't trained for this position, and the longer that the days went on, the more nervous he was becoming. I had to make sure that he didn't panic. He didn't want to part with that million dollars, and I had a feeling that he was going to make sure that he didn't lose it. He was motivated to have both Millie and the million dollars back, and he was unreasonably confident, which

175

meant that he was in the position to do something stupid.

My focus had to be on getting Millie back unharmed, but to do that, I had to keep Chase in check. I was going to talk to Chase at midday tomorrow, take him through the plan step-by-step, and ensure that he wasn't going to go off-script. Casey and I would follow the kidnapper once Millie was safe, and that was our chance to nab the perpetrator.

The phone rang as I pulled into my driveway.

I groaned in frustration; I didn't have time for a phone call right now.

"Jack." It was Chase. He was desperate. "Things have changed. The kidnapper sent another message using another phone number. It's bad."

There was an edge to his voice I hadn't heard before, now he had my attention. I was concerned but it only served to make me more alert.

"How bad?"

I heard Chase take a deep breath, and when he spoke, his voice was shaky.

"The message says that the drop has changed to tonight. Midnight. They need the money on the park bench in four hours or they've threatened to hurt Millie. What are you going to do, Jack?"

"Let's not panic." There was no way this could've been a coincidence. Not even an hour after I had left Tanya's house, and the kidnapper was panicking.

Either Kyle told someone, or he is one mighty fine liar. "What does the message say exactly?"

"It says, 'The drop has changed to midnight tonight. Same location. You bring the money, place it on the park bench, and walk away. You'll see Millie once you've walked away from the bag. The girl gets hurt if you involve the cops or anyone else.'" Chase's voice was high-pitched. He was panicking. "Why have they changed it now? Why aren't they sticking to the original plan?"

I pushed any feelings of guilt away and got down to business. Truth be told, I worked better under pressure anyway.

"This could've been their plan all along. To try and throw anyone off their trail. They want to keep you on your toes." I turned my truck's engine off. "Or they've seen you go to the bank and they know that you've got the money now. Do you remember seeing anyone watching you?"

I got out of the truck and headed into the house as we talked.

"No, Jack. Nobody was watching me. I went to a different bank, just like you said, and I watched my back really closely. I didn't see anyone following me. There was nobody around as I went in, nobody in the bank, and nobody when I came out. I didn't see anyone."

I was strangely calm as I grabbed the leftover pizza. This was going to be a tough night, and I needed something other than beer to get me through it.

"Get ready for the drop. Do everything the kidnapper says. If they send you another text, call me right away," I said. "If not, I'll call you back in one hour."

I hung up the phone, calm but realistic.

This wasn't good. All at once, the investigation had lost a crucial day. Twenty-four hours gone, leaving only four hours to ensure that Millie was safe.

I could sense on the phone that Chase had wanted to talk more, and maybe he needed it. He wanted reassurance, comfort, but right now, he wasn't my concern.

"Casey." I called my assistant. "I need you to call Chase, keep him calm, focused, remind him of his role in the plan. I'm afraid he's going to do something stupid." I paused for a moment before adding the bombshell. "The kidnapper has changed the drop time."

"Why would they do that?" Casey wondered out loud, but she moved on without expecting an answer, "When?"

"Tonight, at midnight," I responded. "Same place, at least."

"Did you manage to get the cameras up?"

"No. I was just on my way over there. We can still go through with the rest of the plan we had. We can still do it tonight. I'll cover the south exit, and you cover the north. If the kidnapper wants to get out of the state as quickly as possible, they'll take the south exit, which is what I'm expecting."

"That seems most likely." Casey agreed. "We'll keep in touch using our phones, but if we get cut off for any reason, I've synced our phone trackers with a sat nav app so we can always trace each other's phones if we need to."

We both went silent. Despite the change of deadline, it suddenly felt like we were back in control of the situation.

"Any closer to figuring out who it might be?" Casey asked.

"Well, I think I can cross two more names off the list of potential kidnappers," I admitted.

Even over the phone, I could sense Casey's surprise.

"Who? How?"

"I stormed into Tanya's house and put a gun to Kyle's head only one hour ago."

"What?" Casey was shocked. "Why?"

"I needed answers." I knew it was a petulant response, but we no longer had the luxury of time to analyze my mistake.

"And just after you stormed into the house, the kidnapper changed the drop time?" I could hear the tension in Casey's voice, she was annoyed. Then suddenly she seemed to have a change of heart, "But that means the kidnapper knows Kyle and Tanya. Or is at least in contact with them. Or it could be one of them and they fooled you."

I felt a small wave of relief, we had a new lead. Time was running out, but suddenly we were back on the kidnapper's trail. I headed back out of the house to my truck.

"You're right. Kyle told me that a stranger had contacted him and informed him that he would be getting his full investment back, all one-hundred thousand dollars. He said that the person would transfer the money to his bank account."

"And you believe him? Or did you think he was covering up the kidnapping? Protecting himself, or Tanya."

"I believed him. People tend to tell the truth with a gun to their head."

That was true. The average person isn't trained to deal with life or death situations, and even though Kyle was a former soldier, he wasn't expecting to answer his front door and have his life threatened. He didn't know me, and he didn't know how dangerous I could be. He assumed the worst, and rightly so.

Kyle had thought that I was a debt collector, and he recognized my face from the truck stop. And I have no doubt that after I left, Tanya recognized my face as well. She would've remembered me from the previous morning at the bar, and that would've scared them both. They knew that I was on their tail, and that I'd been following them.

They would've panicked.

"And so that means that everyone else on that list has probably been told they're going to get their money back?" Casey reasoned. "If what Kyle says is true, then the kidnapper would've contacted the others. Do you need me to get in touch with them, find out what they know? Do we even have time for that?"

That thought hadn't gone through my head, but she was right. If Kyle was contacted, then every one of the people on that list would've been contacted too. But there was only one person I needed to track down now.

If the investors were getting their money back, that included Ben.

And he didn't say a word to me about it.

"I knew there was a reason I kept you around. How far away are you from the office?"

I heard the sound of Casey picking up her car keys.

"I can be there in ten minutes."

"I'll meet you there," I said as I started the engine of my truck. "This investigation isn't over yet."

CHAPTER 23

JUST UNDER four hours until the drop.

Four hours with the life of a young girl on the line. The stakes couldn't have been higher. I raced through the back streets, pushing hard, and every time I passed under a streetlight, the flash of light reminded me of the clock ticking down. As I bounced along the road, I put a call through to Ben. He answered after one ring.

"Why didn't you tell me that someone had contacted you about getting the money back?" I was angry, but calm and calculated. I had to be.

"Jack…" His voice trailed off.

"Ben, you lied to me."

"Jack, listen." As he went to continue, two of his dogs started yapping in the background. "Quiet!" he called out to his dogs. "Jack…"

He said something but I couldn't hear him over the barking.

"I can't hear you, Ben." My patience was growing thin and my anger rising.

"Jack, I didn't plan this. It wasn't me." The dogs continued barking. "Quiet back there! Shut up. Keep

182

it down."

"Who was it Ben?" I yelled into the phone. "Who set this up?! Tell me, damn it!"

"I can't hear you Jack. These dogs are too loud."

I could hear a rustling in the background as Ben tried to get a hold of the dogs and calm them down.

"Who?!" I yelled into the phone. "Who was it, Ben?!"

"I don't know, Jack. Look, I've got to go and feed these dogs." He hung up the phone quickly. Too quickly, like he was using it as an excuse to avoid an unwanted question. To avoid facing the truth.

There was no use calling him back. He wouldn't answer now. He was attending to his dogs. He loved those dogs. Two beagles. Such beautiful animals. He used to enter the beagles into shows, winning awards for Best in Show. They were his life away from policing, probably the only thing that got him through some very hard days. The dogs even had their own social media accounts. Sometimes, his wife complained that he loved those dogs more than he did her, which was probably true, in part. Or perhaps entirely.

Ben had a rough time over the past few years. He lost his father three years ago, his sister, who was my wife Claire, not long after. While still grieving over the lost members of his family, his partner in the police force was shot by gang-bangers in a shoot-out on Chicago's South Side. Nineteen bullets. They said there was practically nothing left of his skull afterwards and they had to identify him through DNA. One of those losses was hard enough, but he suffered each of them just as he was starting to recover from the last.

His dogs, his daughter, and escaping to the river to fish, were about the only things that kept him afloat. But even then, he was a leaky vessel in a constant sea of choppy water.

Did I think he could kidnap a child? Once upon a time I would have said no. Without a doubt. But now. Maybe. Nobody knows what another person is capable of when they're pushed to the edge. And Ben was a man on the edge.

I screeched my truck to the sidewalk in front of my office just as Casey was doing the same. She leapt out of her vehicle, as did I.

"Time until drop?"

"3 hours, 45 minutes." I looked at my watch. "We've got time to solve this before the drop and we have to, because I have a feeling that Chase is going to do something stupid. I can't trust him to follow instructions. That million dollars is worth too much to him."

"I called him, like you asked, and you're right, he's jittery. I did my best to calm him down, keep him focused on what he needs to do, but I'm not sure he was really listening. I got the feeling his mind was on something else. I think he's planning something himself."

I nodded, that was my concern too.

"To be honest, I don't think he really trusted me," Casey continued. "I couldn't get a clear answer from him about anything. Do you know if he has the money ready?"

"He does. Everything is ready to go. He's been instructed to place the money on the park bench at midnight, walk back to the playground, and then they'll release Millie."

"They'll release Millie without checking the bag first?" Casey looked incredulous.

"We're not dealing with professionals. This is someone with a strong sense of justice and good morals. Someone who couldn't conceive risking a child's life over money. The kidnappers would think that Chase would have to be pretty stupid to take that chance. He's not a fighter, and whoever the kidnapper is, they'd know that. They're willing to risk it."

"But you disagree." Casey frowned. "You think he would jeopardize Millie by going back for the money?"

"I do. I'm going to call him back in one hour, take him through step-by-step of what he needs to do. I'm going to go over the risks with him, emphasize the dangers and let him know what can happen if he doesn't play by the kidnapper's rules. And I'm going to be clear: his child will die. And her blood will be on his hands. An indelible stain that he can never wash off."

Without willing it, images started growing in my mind of what would happen if we failed. The headlines screaming about the innocent five-year-old who disappeared when the ransom drop went haywire. Millie's smiling photo next to a picture of Tanya crying.

And possibly the blame being put on me. On the private investigator. The scape goat who Chase would turn on in a heartbeat to save his own reputation and skin. Yeah, that's how it would play out.

Not that I cared about that. I cared about Millie, getting her back without a hiccup. Seeing her safe and well. But with Chase intimately involved in the process, I was understandably concerned.

"And you think you can calm Chase down?"

"No, I don't." We walked into the elevator to the office. "But we don't have a choice."

After the short ride, we entered into the office. Casey sat down at her desk and turned on her laptop.

"How did it go talking to Ben? Anything we can use?"

"He was evasive, but I don't know if that's because he's involved, or because he was looking after his beloved dogs." A thought went through my head. "When you checked the social media accounts around the area, did you check the dog park nearby?"

"I did but there was no information to go on. I

couldn't see anything out of the ordinary. Just photos of smiling, happy dogs."

"Check it again. Bring up the photos. Ben's dogs have social media accounts, so check that location for any pictures of beagles. He posts pictures of those dogs all the time. They used to be show dogs and he's very proud of it. I need to see if he's been in the area at all in the last week, any day."

Casey flicked open the internet browser, typed quickly, and what she found made my mouth drop open.

"Ben's dogs have their own social media accounts, but he doesn't tag their location." Her mouth dropped open as well as she looked at the background in one of the pictures. "But look at this—the last picture was clearly taken in that run-down dog park on the morning that Millie went missing."

<u>CHAPTER 24</u>

İ CALLED Ben's phone back. He didn't answer.

I still couldn't quite believe Ben was involved, but I couldn't hide from the facts. Kidnapper or not, Ben knew more than he was letting on. I felt guilty pursuing Claire's brother, but it wasn't the time to get sentimental. I had to track him down. And if necessary to take him down too.

I tried Ben's phone again. This time, his wife answered.

"Hello, Jack." She sounded cagey.

"Mary, where's Ben? I have to talk to him immediately. It's urgent."

"Sorry, Jack. Ben's not here. He just took off after you called him."

"What do you mean, took off? Where did he go?"

"Is everything alright, Jack? First Ben dashing off, and now you call demanding to know where he is. I mean, I'm kind of used to it, Ben's work often takes him away unexpectedly, but this feels different. More personal somehow. What's going on, Jack? You need to tell me. Is something wrong?"

"Everything's fine. Nothing to worry about." I had

to try and reassure her. The last thing I needed was for Mary to clam up now. I was sure she could help, she must have noticed something, I just needed to get her talking. "We're working on something together and I really need to get in touch with him. I couldn't hear him properly on the phone. He said he was going to call me back, but obviously he's rushed off without his phone. It's urgent, Mary. It needs to be done tonight. Do you have any idea or did he give any indication as to where he was going?"

There was a moment of silence, but I could sense Mary was ready to talk.

"Well, he took another phone call and he seemed quite flustered as he ran out the door. Literally ran. He didn't even say goodbye, he just rushed out of the house and disappeared into the night."

My hand pressed into the table—it was a guilty move, if there ever was one. Only moments after we talked, he ran. I quickly set the phone to speaker so Casey could listen too, in case she picked up on something that I didn't. No matter how small.

"Did he say where he was going? Did he give any indication where he was headed?"

"Not a thing. He barely said a word, and he didn't even take his phone, which is very unlike him," she said. "He doesn't usually leave the house without his wallet, phone and keys."

"So you have no idea where he might be going?"

"Have you tried the station? If he was called into

work, he would usually head there first."

She paused and I almost jumped in with another question to keep her talking, but Casey shook her head and leaned in close to the phone to listen better. Then I heard it too, the jingle of keys in the background.

"Well, that's strange," Mary continued. "Ben's taken my car. He's left his truck in the driveway. He doesn't usually take my car anywhere. He hates to be seen driving around in a Volvo Sedan. I think the guys at work laughed at it once. Called it a grandad car, but really, it's very fuel efficient. Very economical and it's very unusual for him to drive it without me suggesting it."

Casey tugged on my arm, and whispered, "Ask her if the car has a GPS tracker. A lot of modern cars have trackers that can be turned on, generally because a person thinks the car is stolen. But if so, we can track him."

"Mary, does your sedan have a GPS tracker?" I asked.

Mary seemed so surprised that he had taken her car that she had let her guard down. "Oh yes. I think it does. I've never used it, but I've got the app on my phone, if you really need to know where he's headed."

"I need the code, Mary." I grimaced as soon as I had spoken. I had let the urgency back in my voice and I knew this would put Mary back on guard.

"Actually, Jack, I don't know if I should give it to

you." She hesitated. "What if it's official police business that's taken him out of the house so late? That could be confidential work. And there could be a conflict of interest between your work and his."

Casey glared at me and I gave her my most apologetic look. I'd messed up, but I was determined to fix it.

"Mary, do you really think he would have taken your car for official police work? You know he always takes his truck. Ben's in trouble and I'm the only one you can trust to help him. He's in a hole and I'm the one who's gonna dig him out of it. But I can't help if I can't get in touch with him and don't know where he is. I need that code. I need to know where Ben's going. Mary, you have to trust me. And you have to do it right now."

"I don't know, Jack." She was on the edge, and it was time for a touch of the truth.

"Mary, currently there's a young girl's life at stake, and Ben might be walking into a trap." I tried to negotiate with her. "Ben doesn't know it, but there's a five-year-old girl's life on the line."

She paused for a long moment, and I waited.

"A five-year-old girl. What are you talking about? Who is this five-year-old girl? And what's Ben's involvement with her?"

"I can't give you the details but you need to trust me. Come on, Mary. It's me, Jack. Not some stranger. I'm family. And family trusts each other. Trust me now and tell me the code to the tracker."

"I just don't know, Jack."

Casey and I both held our breath. We knew this was make it or break it time.

"Ok, Jack. If you think it's the right thing to do."

"Thank you, Mary. It is."

She then proceeded to give me the log-in details to her car's GPS tracker. I wrote the information down for Casey to see, and she logged it into the account on her laptop.

"It's working. I'm tracking the sedan now." Casey whispered with a thumbs up, as she pointed to a red dot that was flashing on the screen, tracing over the city map.

"Thank you, Mary. Ben will be thankful as well. I promise." I hung up the phone. I could tell that Mary didn't seem convinced, but now wasn't the time to think about the dynamics of my extended family. Plenty of time for that when the night was over. I just hoped I could keep that promise. Time was running out for a happy conclusion.

"Bring that with us." I indicated to the laptop as I began storming out the door. "We'll track it in the car and meet him wherever he's going."

CHAPTER 25

I COULD feel my heart pounding in my ears as I started up the engine on my truck. This was it, the moment that would determine what happened to this case, and to Millie. If I was right, and Ben was involved, then I was hopeful we could save that lovely, little girl's life. But if I was wrong, then this was a big move in the wrong direction and we were out of time. I couldn't live with myself if I let Millie down now in the closing moments of this terrible game. All I could do was hope I was right.

The tracking signal for Ben's car stopped after twenty minutes. Driving my truck, I raced through the streets, the engine screaming for mercy as I pushed hard to get to his position. We were still fifteen minutes away from where he had parked.

I looked at my watch.

Three hours until the drop time.

And I still had to take Chase through the process to make sure that he didn't do anything stupid.

"Where has he stopped?" I quizzed Casey, sitting in the passenger seat with the laptop open in front of her.

"It's not an address I recognize. Let me search the addresses near where the car has stopped." Her fingers typed fast. "Another industrial lot, only thirty minutes away from the drop area. We're closer to the drop area now."

"We've got time. What's in the industrial lot? Any addresses that stand-out?"

"We've got a hardware store, a carpet center, another hardware store, and… ah, a mechanic shop that specializes in diesel mechanics."

My body tingled momentarily as a shot of adrenaline surged through me.

"That's our target. That must be where Ben is going."

I dropped the truck back in gear, roaring it into action, making the fifteen-minute trip in eight. As I turned the corner to the industrial lot, I slowed down, crawling forward, looking for a white sedan in the dimly lit street.

"Are you packing heat?" I turned to look at Casey. She tapped her hip under her jacket.

Slowing the car, I pulled over to the side of the street, switching out the headlights first, and then turning off the engine. My eyes took a moment to adjust to the darkness but even when they did I couldn't see any movement.

We sat for a moment, allowing our eyes to adjust further and taking in the surroundings.

The area around us was dimly lit, with no activity

as the time approached 9pm. There was one other car parked on the street, all the buildings were locked up with extra security, and barbed wire covered the top of the chain fences nearby.

I could see Casey was watching the vehicle intently, so I took a moment longer to look all around. Checking for any signs of movement, anything we should be on guard for. We didn't have a lot of time, but we couldn't afford to rush in and mess it up now.

I was as confident as I could be that we had arrived unnoticed, so I turned my attention to the other car in the street as well.

"White Volvo," I stated.

Casey nodded. "Looks like we've found the car, but no sign of Ben."

"Time for a closer look."

We eased our way out of the truck. I kept the doors well-oiled for moments like this. I couldn't have a creaking door alerting people to our presence.

I indicated to Casey to flank the left side of the sedan and I would flank the right. Jogging in the shadows, we approached the car.

Drawing my piece, keeping it low, I jogged to the side.

I looked in the back window.

Nothing.

Casey, weapon in hand, indicated the same. I looked in the front window.

195

Again, nothing.

Casey shook her head.

I let the breath I had been holding go and indicated we should move forward towards the shadows next to the building.

"The mechanics shop is the third warehouse on the right," Casey whispered. "We'll see it once we go around the next corner."

I led us through the shadows, sticking close to the edge of the wall on the empty street.

I heard the crunch of broken glass under foot behind me and turned to glare at Casey who had frozen in place. With an apologetic look, she cautiously lifted her foot and crept carefully past the remains of a broken bottle. I glanced around nervously, but we were still far enough away from the warehouse to escape notice.

One streetlight was on ahead of us.

I sneaked to the corner, and turned my head around the wall.

The warehouse sat back from the street on a long driveway. There was one long garage door, big enough to fit two trucks side by side, and a workshop door to the right.

"There's a light on in the workshop." I turned back to Casey. "We'll get to the window and see if we can see anything nearby."

Casey strained to see past me without sticking her head out too far. "We'll have to be careful, places like these are bound to have some level of automated security system. Even if they don't have cameras, they'll still have an automatic sensor light."

"There are two cars up the right-hand side of the drive." I looked back around the corner of the wall. "If we stick close to the wall, we have our best chance of staying hidden. On three, we move."

She nodded.

"One, two, three."

We moved quickly, and quietly, sticking to the right hand wall. Reaching the first car under the shroud of darkness, we squatted down.

Ahead of us, I could see movement in the shadows.

It was a figure squatting down behind the second car. I couldn't make out which way they were facing.

I indicated to Casey to cover me.

She raised her weapon, and I moved forward, my steps not making a sound on the concrete. With my gun raised forward, I snuck closer to the shadow behind the next car.

"Ben." My voice was quiet but firm as I looked down at the man squatting low behind the car.

"Jack?" He almost sounded relieved until he turned and saw my gun. He raised his hands. "What are you doing here?"

"Trailing you." My answer was blunt and I stayed in the shadows, a few feet away from him. "And finding a missing girl."

197

"No, Jack, you've got it all wrong." He stayed squatted down, hands still raised. "I'm here to see who's been contacting me."

"You've got one minute to explain yourself." My gun was focused on his torso.

"I… I got a call." He looked to the building in front of us. "I don't know who it was from, but they said they needed my help."

"I know you were at the dog park on Saturday morning, Ben. That's more than a coincidence."

"Ok. Ok." He waved me down. "Look, I don't know who is in that building. All I know is that they needed my help and they sent me a message saying that."

I wanted to believe him, but I knew he still wasn't giving me the whole story.

"Ben. You're family, but that doesn't mean I won't kill you if it saves the life of a little girl. Best you get talking. And don't hold anything back." He could hear the gravity in my voice.

"Alright, Jack." He leaned back down, and rested against the car. "Get lower and I'll tell you everything."

I squatted down, gun still focused on Ben's torso, and indicated for Casey to move forward. She moved forward next to the car, within a foot of Ben. He nodded his hello, more instinct than pleasantry, but she didn't respond.

"I got a message last week saying that if I wanted

my one hundred-thousand-dollar investment back, all I had to do was go to the park, call Chase on a burner phone, and get him angry enough that he would have to walk away from the playground. That's all I was told, and I did it."

"And then?"

He shrugged. "I went to the park with my dogs and watched as Chase arrived with his daughter. I called him at 10am as instructed and pretended I was a potential debt collector looking to find money that he had ripped off from other people. Chase got angry and stepped away from the playground. I kept him on the phone for ten minutes until I received a message simply saying 'hang up', so I did." He paused and looked around.

"Keep talking, Ben," I instructed. This wasn't the time for stalling.

"Ok. I didn't stick around to be seen. As much as I'm sure he wouldn't recognize me anyway, I was just a bank check to him, and we only met once in person, but I couldn't take the risk so I called the dogs over and left. I didn't know that the person was going to kidnap his daughter. I swear it, Jack," Ben added desperately.

"And how do you know that now?" Casey asked.

"When Chase went back to the playground, I watched him from my car, he became slightly frantic, and then he read a text message. He sat on the nearby park bench for ten minutes and then left the playground without his daughter." He shook his head. "That's when I knew something was up. Something wasn't right. I kept an eye on all the police reports, but nothing came up. And then you showed up at my door the next day saying that you were working for Chase, well, I put two and two together from there."

"You didn't raise the alarm?" Casey questioned.

"What could I say? As a cop, I couldn't be involved in a kidnapping. It would be the end of my career. Nobody in the department could know about this. I'd be finished."

"And what about me, Ben. I'm not a cop, you could have come clean to me, but instead you lied to my face. Why? I'm the one person you could have talked to." I glared at him accusingly.

"I thought I could do it myself. I'm a cop, a professional. Tracking down criminals is my job. I never thought I would become an accomplice. Now I'm the criminal, and I've let everyone down. I'm so sorry, Jack."

Well, I wasn't going to disagree.

"And now?" I drew the attention back to our current situation. "Why are you skulking about out here?"

"I got a message from a different number, and they said they needed my help to get the money off Chase. Told me to meet them here at 11pm."

"Who is it?"

"I have no idea. That's why I'm scoping the place

out first." He popped his head over the hood of the car, and looked up to the building. "That's the only light on in the whole industrial park. That's where they want me to meet them."

I raised my gun again. "Then that's where we've got to go. Together."

CHAPTER 26

I QUICKLY glanced at my watch.

Two and a half hours until drop time.

Chase would be getting nervous. He'd be getting worried. The fear would be building, the dread would be consuming his whole body. With time getting short, he would be playing out all the possible scenarios in his head. He'd be looking for an out. An excuse to avoid handing over the money. Any reason he could come up with to hang on to his beloved million dollars and not follow through as we'd agreed. If one thing had been clear from the very start it was this: Chase Martin was not a man who could be trusted, especially when it came to money.

And now it was my turn to consider the options. Was it a greater risk leaving Chase to drop the money, than it would be to charge into the warehouse all guns blazing?

If this went wrong, and it easily could, all would be lost.

It was decision time.

I looked at the looming warehouse, with its single light shining like a beacon to those who were adrift.

In truth, I felt lost. Torn about which way to turn and what course of action to follow. But life is full of difficult decisions and sometimes you just have to flip a coin.

It was dark enough to cover the run to the door, so long as there were no security lights. My eyes strained in the dark, and then I saw it, the pinpoint flash of red above the door. I nudged Casey and gestured towards it.

I could see her studying the light sensor and our possible approach to the door, before she whispered her response.

"If we stay wide until we hit the wall over there," she pointed to the nearest corner of the building, "and then shadow the wall, we should avoid the sensor. I hope," she added.

I nodded as I weighed out the situation. I trusted Casey. No question. I trusted myself. I even trusted Ben, if not for his personal decisions, I trusted his police skills. He was a good cop, and I knew it.

And finally, I trusted my gut.

What I didn't know was, could I trust Chase?

If the kidnapper didn't know who Chase was, I would've been the one placing the drop, but clearly they knew him. They would have known if I tried to replace him.

If I backed out of raiding the warehouse now, we would have to go back to the original plan. The only other plan we had. And that meant I would have to trust Chase with the drop.

And as much as I tried, I couldn't place my faith in Chase.

Not even with his own daughter's life on the line. There was an arrogance to him, a feeling that he deserved every cent of that money. Not to mention that he ripped people off for the money in the first place, but he felt it was rightfully his. And sometimes people fight even harder to keep hold of what they've stolen than what they've earned through sweat and toil.

It was the game he played.

Money was everything to men like him. It was the validation that he sought, making him feel worthy, powerful and successful. In my eyes, he wasn't successful. He was immoral. A fraudster. A cheat. A loser. No matter how much money he had in the bank. I couldn't do what he did. I couldn't live the life that he leads.

And so, the decision was made.

From right now, Chase was not my concern.

It was the warehouse, who was in it, and how long we had until they left. The warehouse was a half hour drive to the drop, and that meant the kidnapper would be leaving soon. I had no doubt that the kidnapper would scope the drop first, looking for any unmarked cop cars, or for anything unusual.

We had minutes, not hours, until the kidnapper made a move.

Under my lead, Ben, Casey and I continued in the shadows until we reached the edge of the warehouse. Our guns were drawn, our heart rates high, and our determination unquestionable. Apart from the tall garage doors, there was one entrance, a metal door that led into the office, and one small window. With Ben and Casey behind me, we moved to our positions under the window. Easing out of my crouched position, I looked inside.

There, on a couch, was Millie Martin.

Relief flooded through me, but we certainly weren't done yet.

She was sleeping, wrapped up nicely in a blanket, her head resting on a pillow. She had been laid down with care—there wasn't a scratch on her, not a mark. She was resting like the little angel she was.

"She's in there." I leaned back down against the wall. "Millie is sleeping on a couch, only a few feet from the door. She looks unharmed, and peaceful."

We took a moment for this information to process.

"Anyone else?" Ben checked his weapon. "No other activity?"

I shook my head, "Not that I could see."

Ben slowly stood and looked in the window. "To the back of the room is another door." He leaned back down. "There's light coming from it. The kidnapper must be in the other room."

I nodded as Ben crouched back down next to

Casey.

"This is the plan." I indicated to Casey and Ben. "I'm going to pick the lock, enter the room first, and keep my gun on that other door. The two of you are going to follow me inside, and carry Millie out of there. And I don't want a sound coming from her mouth."

"I'll carry her," Casey said. "I can do it gently."

"And I'll stick with you, Jack."

"No, Ben. I need you to cover Casey and Millie. Casey will have her hands full, so she won't have her weapon drawn. I need you to cover her all the way back to the car. If things go wrong for me in there, then Casey and Millie will still have coverage."

"What are you going to do?"

"I'm going to cover that door until the three of you are down the driveway, and then I'm going to put an end to this sordid business once and for all."

"But you don't even know how many people are in there, Jack," Casey stated. "You don't know anything about what's beyond that door."

She was right. I didn't know. I didn't know how many people were there, I didn't know how many guns they had, and I didn't know what I was walking into. I didn't know if it was ten armed professionals, or one lonely soul.

But I wasn't going to risk Millie's life. I was going to see this through to the end.

Keeping low, I snuck to the door, tested it and

found it was locked. It was easy to pick the old lock, and I was able to open it within a few seconds. Casey placed her weapon in the gun belt, clipped it, and then she and Ben crept over to the door.

Ben got in position to open the door, and Casey waited behind me. It was time to rock and roll. To kick ass and take names.

I counted down to three on my fingers.

Three.

Two.

One.

Quietly, Ben turned the door open, and I stepped into the room without a sound, gun pointed forward. My footsteps were silent as I scanned the room.

The room was sparse, just a couch, a television, and an old desk to the left.

"Clear," I whispered.

Casey followed me in and I crossed the floor to the far end of the couch, putting myself between the kidnapper and Millie. Ben waited by the door, covering the exit.

I kept my weapon focused on the back door, ready to fire the second the handle turned.

Casey leaned down, tucked her hands underneath Millie, and gently raised her up. She kept the blanket around her, trying to keep the movements minimal. Millie stirred, but then leaned into Casey's shoulder.

Casey turned and walked out, and Ben eased the door closed behind them, his weapon still drawn.

Out of the window of the office, I watched as Casey carried the still sleeping Millie safely out of harm's way, with her head resting on Casey's shoulder, under the coverage of Ben who still had his gun drawn. They moved to the side of the driveway, under the protection of the shadows. They passed the two cars, moving towards the end of the road. They were hurrying, but cautious not to attract the attention of any sensor lights. I watched the shadows closely, watching them move, and kept my hearing focused on any movement from the other side of the door. I could hear a murmur, but no movement.

Once Casey, Millie and Ben were safely past the end of the driveway, I turned my focus back to the room I was in. There was very little I could do if this turned into a gun fight. If I had to, I could get behind the couch and it would provide some protection for a short while, not protection from bullets, they'd pass through it easy enough, but protection from view, perhaps long enough to get a few shots fired before I was spotted, but I didn't know if that would be enough. It all depended on how many people were in that room and how hostile they were.

I almost hoped the door would open, and bring the fight to me. Once I crossed the floor to it, I would be exposed and vulnerable.

Whatever happened now, I had done my job, and that innocent child was on her way back to where she belonged.

But for me, this wasn't over yet.
It was time to open that door.

CHAPTER 27

I STARED at the door for a long moment, waiting for it to open. If it moved, I'd pump it full of bullets, retreat, reload and then come back to pump it full of more bullets. Technically this would be murder. I had no idea who was in there or whether they posed an immediate threat, so in a court of law I'd be convicted sure enough. But morally they deserved it. And that's what mattered to me. Whoever was on the other side of that door was a criminal, a person who wanted to risk the life of a little girl for money. Thank goodness Millie was now safe, but that didn't change who I was about to face when I entered the next room.

A kidnapper.

The worst sort. I had no idea what Millie had been through over the past few days. Was she frightened? Did the experience scare her or would it permanently scar her? Had her entire life been changed by the last five days?

Those were questions that I didn't know the answer to, but I was sure to find out. Whoever was on the other side of that door wanted money, and they were willing to do anything to get it.

Money. I had contempt for what it led people to do. I only wanted as much as I needed. Beyond that was greed, and look what that led to. People like Chase. Situations like this. Evil. Endangering an innocent little girl's life, for what?

I took one last look around the dimly lit room I was standing in and took a deep breath—there was nothing to suggest that the person on the other side of the door was a killer. There wasn't even a bit of trash on the floor. But that didn't tell me who I was about to meet. They said Hitler was meticulously neat, just look at that moustache, that he loved animals and was a vegetarian, so appearances didn't always tell the whole picture. I had to be prepared for anyone.

There was a noise from the other side of the closed door, subdued and humming. A television show, perhaps.

I crept forward and put my ear to the door. I thought maybe I heard a quiet chuckle, but maybe it was just the television. I didn't want to get too relaxed, it could be an ambush waiting for me, guns blazing all around. But at least Millie was safe. Now it was just me and my future. I'd never been too sure about my fate. If this was it, then so be it.

I eased my hand onto the cold metal door handle and carefully tested the door. It opened.

I took a deep breath, and slowly, I pushed it further open.

It opened silently into the workshop and I felt a

rush of cool air on my face.

My gun was drawn in front of my eyes, my steps soft as I moved towards the humming noise. As I stepped inside the workshop, I could see the light was coming from an old television across the other side of the room. There was a truck between me and the television, and I moved around it carefully.

The warehouse was at least two floors tall and the lighting was almost non-existent. It was cold and the dank air smelled of diesel. Looking around the room, I saw a calendar of naked women over my left shoulder pinned up by the door next to a row of key hooks. On my right there was a pile of dirty work clothes next to a greasy looking sink. Plenty of work tools around, but all neatly placed on benches or hanging on the wall, so no danger of tripping at least.

Being careful not to make a sound, I gently stepped forward. With my weapon focused ahead, I pointed it at where the light was coming from. My heart was pounding in my ears as I neared the corner of the truck, from where the kidnapper would be revealed.

As I stepped around the truck, I saw the shadow of a person sitting on a chair, staring at the light coming from the television, watching an old show quietly. The person was sitting in an armchair, almost sinister enough to be the armchair of a Bond villain. The television was sitting on two milk crates, a makeshift table for viewing pleasure.

I stepped closer, keeping near to the truck for cover.

It was a male.

The man was leaning back in the chair, relaxed, totally engrossed in the comedy show. The noise was down low and again I heard a low laugh, soft as though he was stifling it, probably so as not to wake Millie in the other room.

I came within a few feet.

My finger was poised on the trigger, every muscle in my body was tensed for action.

I was ready to pump the person full of bullets with one false movement. I glanced around the workshop as I cleared the safety of the truck, but it was dark and still. We were alone, I was certain of that.

I stepped closer. Then I sighed.

The noise made the man snap his head around, his eyes focused directly on my gun.

I could see the panic in his eyes as he flicked his gaze to the open office door. He was wondering about Millie, what had happened to her.

His look was alarmed as he stared back at me and my gun. It took him a moment, and then he recognized me.

"They must take school applications very seriously these days," he quipped. "You've really done your research."

Then five bullets rang past my ear.

CHAPTER 28

THE SOUND of gunshots was deafening. As soon as Damon Hardy's hand moved, I dove to my left, taking cover behind the nearest vehicle. I crawled on my stomach as the shots continued.

"Damon!" I called out. "It doesn't have to be like this!"

I sat up, leaning against a tire, hearing the sound of his handgun being reloaded.

"Damon!" I called out again. "Stop this."

There was silence. The truck didn't provide much shelter. I was a sitting duck. I checked my gun, it was ready, but I didn't want to pull the trigger. No doubt, Damon would think that I was one of Chase Martin's hired guns. In a way, he was right. Chase had employed me, but that didn't stop me from having a heart.

I leaned down and looked under the truck, searching in the dim light for any movement. The smell of gasoline filled the air, and I knew every shot was a risk. One loose shot, one stray bullet, and it would send the place sky-high. That wasn't the best choice for anyone.

I heard a noise to my left. I turned sharply, searching the shadows for any further movement.

"Damon," I called out again. "Talk to me."

There was another sound. A squeak. He was circling me. Moving to a better position. He was a trained professional in an environment that he knew well, and I was an open target.

I stood and began moving to my left, inching away from the truck, gun ready to fire in return.

Another noise to my left. I kept low.

A shot fired. The slug whizzed past my ear. I could hear the fizz of the bullet. I dove behind a stack of cardboard boxes as another shot rang out.

"Damon!"

I stood, gun focused in the direction of the fire. In the dark edges of the workshop, I searched for any movement.

Another sound. To my right.

I swung the gun to focus in that direction. I saw another movement. He was near the truck. Near the smell of gasoline.

"Damon! Stop this!"

I couldn't shoot. If I hit the gas, the whole place could go up, killing myself and Damon in the process. I lowered down, moving around the tool bench at the edge of the room.

I caught sight of Damon. He was standing behind the truck, the gun still focused on the boxes where I was standing. He hadn't seen me move.

I had the upper hand, but one stray shot meant the whole place would explode.

Moving softly, I stepped around the back of the vehicle, past the couch, hiding in the shadows.

I moved within ten feet, my gun focused on the back of his head. He was searching the shadows near the boxes for me.

"Drop the weapon," I said. "It's over."

He turned sharply. He had no intention of surrendering.

I lunged at his right wrist, pushing the gun away from us.

Two more shots rang out.

The smell of gasoline was overwhelming.

I struggled to get the gun free. Another shot.

Then another.

I pushed his arm towards the sky, stretching him out.

The gun dropped free, and I cracked his jaw with my left elbow.

He fell hard.

With my gun focused on his face, I kicked his gun further from reach.

With desperate eyes, he looked up at me. "Did Chase employ you to kill me?"

CHAPTER 29

"STAY STILL." I kept my gun focused on him.

He didn't move. Keeping his eyes closed, he spoke. "Where's Millie?"

Damon Hardy looked worn out. His eyes looked heavy, his skin looked dehydrated and his face looked sunken.

Life and illness had taken its toll.

"She's safe, Damon," I reassured him. "I made sure of that."

He looked at me with disgust.

"She was always safe," he replied, with a hard edge to his voice. "Do you really think I would have hurt her?"

With heavy movements, he rolled to his side and then climbed to his feet.

"Don't make any sudden moves." I warned him.

He stopped in his tracks. "I'm too old to make sudden movements," he responded with a sad laugh, then he turned back to look at me. He looked at the television, still humming with a quiet sound. "I don't have long left, you know?"

He walked to the old television set and turned it

off. He was past worrying about me and what I might do. He was a man at the end.

He tried to smile as he moved back to the chair and sat down with a sigh. "So that's it then? Chase has got Millie back, and we all walk away, back to our normal lives."

I frowned and shook my head.

"It's not that simple."

Damon looked at me questioningly.

"Isn't it? I didn't kidnap Millie. She's my granddaughter. We've had a lovely time together. Far nicer than she has with that excuse for a father of hers. I didn't harm a single hair on that girl's head. She's my angel, you know. I would do anything for my Millie. She's so sweet, so lovely, and so, so beautiful." He shook his head. "I wish I could be here to see her grow up. I wish I could see her live her life."

"You'll have to do that from behind bars."

"Behind bars?" He smiled. "But I didn't kidnap her."

"But you did try and take the ransom from Chase. That's a crime. He'll press charges. And he'll win. You'll spend the rest of your life in a federal facility."

He sighed once more and turned away from me. It was a few more moments before he continued. His breathing was arduous.

"I'll be dead before the trial even takes place. The doctor said I've got a few months, at most. And I can feel it, I can feel all the strength draining from me. I'm a shell of the man I used to be. I used to be strong and proud, and now I'm skinny and weak. I could barely pick Millie up. That's not the man I want her to remember me as. I don't want her to come to the hospital and look at her weak grandfather. I don't want her to pity me and I don't want that to be the lasting memory she has of me." His head drooped. "I need that angel to remember me as a strong man who fought for his country, who worked hard, and as someone who fought for his family, no matter the cost."

"Is that what this is?"

He turned his head quickly back to me. "Do you think it's fair that Chase makes all the money, and the people that risk their lives for this country are broke? I risked my life for the United States of America, for all who live in this great country, even for people like Chase, and I have nothing. Nothing. I have nothing to leave Millie. Not a cent. And Kyle and Tanya, well, they lost everything they had in one of Chase's schemes. Of course, Chase doesn't pay for it, does he? He still gets to live in his nice penthouse, he still gets his commissions. But us hard working people, the people that make this country work, we get nothing. It's always that way. Do you think that's fair?"

I didn't answer, but Damon wasn't looking for an answer. He was looking for a way to explain the situation he was in. To justify kidnapping his own granddaughter.

"I have nothing to give to Millie. Nothing." His voice was beginning to break down with emotion. "This ransom was my way of giving Millie something. I was going to give it all back to the people that lost their money in Chase's criminal scheme. Those who are still alive that is. You know some of them are dead because of what he did? One guy, a loner, died by suicide. He had no family to give the money to. I was going to leave that portion of the funds to Millie. I could have helped the other people he stole from—including Kyle and Tanya—and then have a little bit to leave as a trust fund for Millie. A present from her grandfather, something to be proud of and something to remember me by."

I could see what he was trying to do. But I had to remain cold. I was here to rescue a little girl, and to protect Chase's money. That was what I was hired to do. I couldn't be moved by Damon's sob story. Whatever his reasons, what he did was still a criminal act, and nothing either of us said or did now could change what had happened.

My response was blunt. "It's a bit late for leaving her something now."

"You think I haven't tried my whole life?" Damon finally let the anger out. "I went to war, I came back and worked sixty hours a week for thirty years. I owned a home, a business and investments, but we

220

lost all that in the financial crisis. We lost everything. When I lost my wife, I had nothing else. I even had to rent a tiny apartment that was falling apart. I worked hard my whole life and I had nothing to leave my angel."

I lowered my weapon as I watched a single tear run down Damon's cheek.

He was a strong man, but he had reached his limit.

Damon wasn't a threat.

Not to me, and certainly not to Millie.

"I just needed to leave her something, you know? I thought if I could just leave her with some money, she could be more independent when she grows older. Even with that prick of a father, she's going to grow up to be a wonderful woman. I know that. I can sense it. She's a good person, a really great person. With so much potential."

I stepped forward and rested my hand on his shoulder.

"Chase is an evil man. He deserves to go to prison, not me." Damon continued. "He's the one breaking the law every month, every day, ripping off innocent people like Kyle, and all the others that were part of the investment group."

"You wanted to give the money back to them. How did you find them all?"

He snorted. "I know Chase, he's lazy. After the easy buck. I knew a couple of people who had invested with him and I figured they would all be linked somehow. A nephew here, a friend there. I managed to find most of them in the end. Not like I have much else to do. Even got one of those nice volunteers at the local library to help with the internet searches, I'm not much good with modern technology, but I just told them I was reaching out to my extended family before I died and they were happy to help. There are still decent people in the world. People who will help a friend in need. Especially one who, like them, has nothing. Why is it always those who have the least that are the ones who give the most?"

He shook his head and smiled.

I had just one more question.

"But how did you know Chase had ripped them off? How did you find out it wasn't just a normal investment gone wrong?"

"When I went to pick up Millie one day, I overheard Chase on the phone talking about what he did to those men. He set up fake companies in other countries, and then took the money. It was a scam. It was all a scam. I took that information to the police, but they said they didn't have enough to charge him with it. All the companies were outside of their jurisdiction. He's the real criminal. Not me."

"Was there any evidence?"

"It's all there." Damon gestured to a messy pile of papers on the desk. "I can't afford to pay you, you know that, but I think you're an honest person. I have a feeling about you. I'd appreciate it if you would take the information and see if you can do anything to help those poor people that Chase ripped off. There's nothing more I can do now. I gave it my best shot. And it would've worked had it not been for you, Mr. Valentine. I guess in the end you were just too good for me. You've got your man and you've solved the case. But please, grant this old dying man a final wish, take a look at those papers and see what you can do to help those people. Those who need it most."

I thought for a few moments before nodding. It was the least I could do.

I gathered up the papers before continuing.

"Sir, it's time to go."

He forced another smile, and then stood proudly. He led me out of the door, and I couldn't help but feel heartbroken for the man. He was a hero, a hard worker, an honorable person, and he had been ripped off by people like Chase Martin. He had been ripped off by life. And this was all that was left for him.

I walked out with Damon in front of me but as we stepped out of the front door, he stopped.

There was a light rain falling now, refreshing and cleansing after the tension of the day.

"I forgot my jacket." Damon turned to me, a tear in his eye. He was shaking slightly. "Do you mind if I go back inside the workshop and get it?"

I knew what that meant.

I knew there was no jacket.

I nodded, and he turned.

"Wait." I stopped him and held out my hand to shake his. "Thank you for your service to our country."

He hesitated, and then shook my hand with all the strength he had left. It was a frail grip, but one filled with pride.

He gave me a nod, pulled his shoulders back, and walked back into the warehouse.

I didn't wait. I began walking down the driveway, back towards the car.

As I took my phone out of my pocket, ready to call Casey, the sound of a gunshot snapped through the silent night.

I sighed and hung my head.

Turning back to the dark building and with a heavy heart, I made the sign of the cross.

"Damon Hardy. May you rest in peace."

<u>CHAPTER 30</u>

WHEN I returned to the office, Millie was sitting on an office chair, headphones over her ears, staring at the glowing screen of an IPad. She looked calm and relaxed, like she'd just spent a week on vacation. Her hair was perfectly brushed, her clothes were clean, and her eyes had a sparkle in them.

Casey stared at me when I walked in. "What happened?"

I nodded to Millie, seeing if she could hear us, and Casey shook her head. "She's fine," she whispered. "Millie said that she'd been hanging out with her grandfather for a week. She has no idea what's happened. We had to make up a reason why we took her in the middle of her sleep."

Casey sat next to Millie for a moment, said something to her, and Millie happily responded, completely unaware of the tragedy in her life. Casey indicated to the room next to us, and I walked in. Casey followed a minute later.

The meeting room felt cold, empty, with a vast confusion filling the air. The boardroom table was still filled with piles of evidence we'd been gathering, file upon file of potential suspects. I looked at the names, and shook my head. The list of people that Chase Martin had conned was long, and up until a week ago, he was untouchable.

"Ben went out for supplies for Millie. He'll be back in ten minutes," Casey said as she checked on Millie once more, then shut the door behind her. "Millie had no idea about any of this. She thinks that she's just had a happy week with her grandfather. That's all. She was so confused as to why we were taking her away from him. I made up a story that Damon had gotten ill and was taken to the hospital, so we had to look after her until her parents arrived in the morning. She seemed to believe that."

"That's good, Casey." I leaned against the table in the boardroom, dropping my head to stare at the floor. "You did well."

"She's happy at the moment, just playing games on the IPad. That'll keep her entertained for the next hour or so." She lowered her voice. "What happened? Where's Damon?"

"He shot himself."

"Oh." Casey's hand went to her mouth. "That's not good."

"No, Casey, it's not good," I said. "He was dying of cancer, and all he wanted was to leave something behind for Millie. That's all he wanted. That's what all this was about. All Damon wanted was for Millie to have a happy life."

Casey folded her arms and nodded. "So what happens now?"

"We call Chase and tell him that we've found Millie."

"That's not right, Jack. We can't let Chase have her," Casey complained. "There's something wrong about this. We know that man has ripped people off, we know that man is a crook, and we're letting him get away with it."

"We're paid to do a job, Casey. I'm not going to change that."

"But it's not right," she pleaded. "Why should Chase get away with ripping off all those people? People have died because of what he did. He's pushed people to suicide. This isn't right."

"It will be right when Chase pays us."

"You don't believe that." Casey snapped back. "You don't believe that at all."

I avoided eye contact. I hated to admit it, but she was right. I sighed heavily and looked to the floor. I shook my head as I began to pace the room. I was heartbroken for Damon, and all the other people Chase had conned, but they didn't employ me. Chase Martin was paying the bills. I had to remember that. I walked over to the whiteboard, and looked at the names on it. We had a list of suspects in the case, a list of potential kidnappers, and we'd already crossed Damon off.

"He didn't kidnap anyone, did he?" I questioned.

"No, Damon Hardy was spending time with his granddaughter," Casey said. "So, what are we going to do?"

"We have one play left," I conceded. "But it's very, very risky."

CHAPTER 31

FIVE MINUTES until drop.

I was parked in my truck, watching the scene for any sign of a giveaway. The rain had cleared from earlier, giving everything a fresh feel as if the air itself had been washed clean. I had a perfect view of what I needed to see, the park, the bench where the drop was to be made, and of Chase.

Chase was ready, waiting at the edge of the park. Even in the dark, I could see he was edgy, shifting his weight from one foot to the other, wanting to pace but I'd told him not to move from that spot until I gave him the word. Dressed in black, he had the bag in his left hand, a small knife in his right. He didn't own a gun. Never even had fired one. He said that he never trusted himself with them and didn't want them in his house. I didn't try to talk him out of taking the knife, even though I knew it was a bad idea, he would have done it anyway, and at least this way I was prepared for what he might do.

We had talked earlier and I told him to keep calm. I told him to focus on his breath when things seemed overwhelming. I repeated over and over that no amount of money was worth the life of his daughter. He looked confused at first, but after thirty minutes of talking, he reluctantly agreed with my point of view. I'd set him up with an earpiece, and I had the microphone clipped to the top of my shirt. To reassure him, to make sure he kept to the plan, and to try and prevent him from bolting into the night with the cash.

I informed him that we were dealing with dangerous people. People that were willing to kill for the money. To kill Millie but also kill him. Chase was scared, no doubt about that, but he was most fearful of losing the money he illegitimately gained. We had never talked about the details of his business, we never talked about how he raised the money to live the lifestyle he lived. It was clear to me all along that he was corrupt, it was clear that he didn't have a moral bone in his body, but that didn't matter because the life of an innocent girl was at stake. Millie Martin had never done anything wrong, never betrayed anyone, and she didn't deserve to be punished for her father's immoral deeds.

Chase's evasion of the FBI was a clear indication of how deeply his corrupt business ran. He must've known that the longer he played with fire, the more likely he was to get burned. The longer he played the game, the higher the chances that he would lose. The house always wins.

The park was empty, as expected. There were no

children running around, no mothers chasing little ones, and there were no dogs barking in the distance. The moon was dim and low in the sky, the glow from the city lights drowning out any chance to see any stars. A drunk homeless man had rested on a park bench earlier that night, but I gave him a fifty and told him to move along. He looked excited, like it was the most money he had ever seen, and he happily walked out of the park. I was concerned he might've been a cop, but then Chase would never have called them. Especially at this late stage.

It was time.

The bell was about to toll.

Chase's hand shot up to his ear as I spoke, and I had to remind him that it was a giveaway that he was wearing an earpiece. I told him to relax. To act natural. But his natural state was a constant paranoia and suspicion. He judged the world by his own morality. To him the world was full of people like him. People who wouldn't hesitate to take advantage of him for their own good.

"Walk up to the bench, place the bag on the bench, and walk straight back here. Don't stop, don't even pause. Look straight ahead at all times, we don't want to spook anyone."

Chase nodded slightly, but I could see his face just well enough to know that he was considering other options. He was imagining a fight for the money. Of pulling out his knife and making a futile last stand. I had to hope he would do as asked. I told him I couldn't have him endangering Millie. That he should focus on her and work to keep her safe at all times.

Under the darkness of the night, I watched as Chase moved towards the park bench, looking over both shoulders, looking for any movement in the park. I had considered giving him a microphone as well, but decided against it as I didn't need to hear any more whining about how much money he was about to lose. I'd already heard too much of that talk. Tonight he would have to remain silent for once and simply follow orders.

He stepped towards the designated drop area, close to the sidewalk on the other side of the park, and reached to place the bag on the bench. He hesitated as if some unseen force was imploring him to hold onto the bag.

"Put the bag down, Chase. Put it down, right now!" I commanded through his earpiece.

With a frustrated sigh he placed it down on the bench but his grip held strong. He didn't move for a few moments, still holding the bag, not wanting to leave that amount of money alone in the park.

"Let go, Chase!"

Finally, he stepped back. Scowling across the park, looking under trees and into the dark recesses of bushes, searching out the hidden location of the unseen recipient of the ransom.

But still he waited, much too close to the bag,

almost within arms' reach.

"Move back," I said from inside my truck, parked across the road, staring at the night.

Against my earlier advice, Chase pushed his finger in his ear. He heard the instructions through his earpiece, I could see his reluctance, but he moved back a few steps. Not far enough.

"Further," I spoke into the microphone. "You're too close. You need to move back to the other side of the playground as planned. Get away from the bag, Chase. Move away from the bench."

He hesitated and I could see his grip tighten on the knife in his hand.

"Chase, your daughter's life is at stake. You need to move back further. You mustn't put her at risk."

Still, he hesitated, but after a few moments he moved.

As soon as he had reached the other side of the park, a van pulled up to the sidewalk close to the bench. Chase took a step forward, ready to confront whoever was in there. The van slowly started to move again.

"Hold on," I warned him. "We don't even know if Millie is in there yet and if they see you move, they will leave. This will all be over and you will never see Millie again."

Reluctantly, Chase stepped back again.

Still with its engine running, the van came to a complete stop.

We waited. I was conscious that I was holding my breath, but this was the make or break moment.

Millie stepped out of the back of the van.

For a moment, she looked around confused, and then she saw Chase.

"Daddy," she cried out with joy.

She ran towards her father.

Chase went to move.

"Don't move! Wait for her to come to you. They may be armed. This is not over yet."

Millie reached Chase and threw her arms around his legs. He gave her a quick rub on the arms then moved her behind him, his eyes on the bag the whole time.

Chase was itching to go for the bag.

Within seconds, before Chase could react any further, I instructed his next moves.

"Get out of the park!" I yelled into my microphone. "And get in my car!"

I saw him look first at Millie and then towards the bag.

I could almost hear him shout, 'What about the money?' but that shouldn't have been his concern and it certainly wasn't mine.

"Get to the car, Chase! Or this will not end well!" I shouted again, and roared my truck to life, pulling to the curb near Chase. "Keep your daughter safe!"

No one else got out of the van. It sped off into the night before anyone could grab the bag.

The black bag was still on the park bench.

Millie was hugging her father's legs.

I could sense Chase's hesitation; I could see his reluctance. Roaring the truck in first gear, I drove over the sidewalk and onto the grassed area of the park.

"Get in the truck!" I yelled at him through the window. "Get Millie into the truck!"

He looked at me, then to his daughter hugging his leg, and then back to the bag. The bag was twenty yards away, close enough for a sprint.

"Don't do it, Chase!" I roared the accelerator of my truck. "Ignore the bag and get into the truck!"

"What about my money?" He yelled as Millie started crying. "We can't leave it there!"

Just then headlights rounded the corner and approached the park.

"They're coming for it, Chase!" I yelled. "If you go for it now, you'll get shot! We have to leave! Now!"

He took one last look at the money, and then turned to the truck. Picking Millie up, he ran the few yards and placed Millie on the backseat before scrambling in after her.

In that instant, I roared the accelerator of my truck, spinning the tires, and sped away down the street almost before he had even closed the door.

"What about my money? Where is Casey? Is she keeping an eye on it?" He pleaded with me.

"Casey is doing her job." I turned sharply around a

235

corner. "Right now, our focus is getting Millie out of here."

Chase looked over his shoulder as we drove away. Millie hugged him tight, but his eyes were on the park as we sped down the road.

We'd left the bag there. We'd left the money behind.

All one million dollars.

CHAPTER 32

FIVE DAYS after the intense night, five days after the drop, I sat in my office, feet up on my table, sipping on a glass of whiskey. It was early in the day but so what. Winston Churchill used to have a daily 'whiskey mouthwash' in the morning. And if it was good enough for him then it was good enough for me. He once said, 'When I was younger I made it a rule never to take a strong drink before lunch. It is now my rule never to do so before breakfast.' Quite right, too. Mine was a glass of Basil Hayden's, my favorite spirit, a lighter-bodied bourbon. A buttery flavored whiskey with a smooth finish, it was liquid gold, a perfect punch of alcohol and aroma. One of life's little pleasures and one I felt was well earned.

It had been a crazy two weeks but I was feeling uncharacteristically relaxed.

I sat at my desk reading a second-hand book I picked up that morning, a book by Agatha Christie. A real five star read. The pages were worn, the writing faded, but the story remained the same—a gripping, page-turning and fabulous tale of a private detective. There was no doubt that Hercule Poirot was the greatest investigator in literary history. I read many of those stories as I was growing up, and I often hoped that I would arrive at a remote five-star hotel, where we were snowed in, and one of the guests was murdered during the night. I would gather up the ten other people staying at the hotel, and systematically work out who the killer was in the luxurious surroundings. As a Private Investigator, that was my dream, but mostly, I had to settle for the cut and dried world of crime and betrayal in Chicago.

To work on something like a kidnapping, a case where I was personally invested in the outcome, was the spark that lit my fire. I didn't sleep for more than five hours over those days, too anxious to rest, too desperate to save Millie from any horrible fate.

Casey and I did that, of course.

We saved Millie.

Not that I ever thought that Damon would've harmed Millie. She was always safe in his care. She went back to her mother's house the day after the drop.

I convinced Chase not to question Millie, to prevent further trauma, and she would speak to him when she was ready. And for his part, I think he felt enough guilt not to want to bring it up.

Millie told Casey about the days she had spent with her grandfather, laughing, playing games and watching old television movies. Apparently, Damon wanted to introduce Millie to the cartoons of his youth—and she spent the bulk of the week watching Disney movies from the fifties. All the while eating her favorite mint chocolate chip ice cream.

Damon's body was found the next day when the workers arrived—an unfortunate suicide, they ruled it. It was more euthanasia, I would've argued, but that isn't in our law books. The funeral was in two days, and I wasn't sure that Chase would attend.

Chase paid my fee, fifty-thousand as promised, but he wasn't happy about it. He sent me a five-page email about how my services were highly overrated, and that while he got his daughter back unharmed, he still lost his money. He said that if I was half the investigator that he'd been led to believe, then not only would he have got his daughter back, but it would have been without losing a single cent.

Taking a sip of my whiskey at the chapter break of my book, I leaned back in my chair and drew a deep breath.

I was still waiting for the penny to drop.

I had expected Chase to storm into our office and verbally abuse me days ago, but he clearly hadn't put it all together yet. It was counting down to almost five full days past the event, and he still hadn't put together all the pieces of the puzzle.

The news of Hugh Guthrie's release from prison was still getting under my skin, but I knew I had to take my time with him. I couldn't go in all guns blazing. That wouldn't work. I would have an opportunity to take him down. I knew that. I just had to wait for my chance.

I turned back to my book with a little shake of my head, but I didn't get far.

Hearing the front door of the office slam shut, I smiled. I relished a good confrontation and the moment had come. Finally, Chase had managed to connect the dots. At just after 10am, he stormed into the office, ignoring Casey at the front desk, and charging straight through my open door.

"What the hell?!"

It was more of a statement than a question, so I didn't respond, barely lifting my eyes up from my book.

"Millie just told me that she spent five days with Damon and that a woman named Casey helped her into the van!" He spat the words at me.

"And?" I reached across and sipped my whiskey, savoring the dance of grain on my tongue.

"That's your assistant!"

"And?"

"And you stole my money! You set me up from the start!"

"I never stole a cent of your money." I stood from behind my table. "You left one million dollars unattended on a park bench. Who knows who found that money? I don't know who took the bag. We didn't have time to set up the cameras, remember?"

"You took the money." He tried to look

intimidating. "And I'll prove it."

"Go ahead." I picked up my phone and put it within his reach. "The FBI deals with situations like this. I'm sure they would love to talk with you."

He hesitated, then stepped back. He had no recourse and suddenly didn't know what to do next. This was not going according to his plan.

"You've set me up. You've ripped me off." The shock was written all over his face. "Why? Just because some idiots invested in the wrong company?"

I would've loved to have argued with him, but there would've been no use. People like Chase Martin are so convinced of their actions, their own power, that nothing could sway them from what they did. They lied to the world and then they lied to themselves. Who knows what they really believed.

Kyle got his money delivered to his account, as the kidnapper had promised, as did everyone else from the investment group. Even the wife of one of the deceased investors. Damon had left all the information we needed, including bank account details, in the file he gave me.

There was one investor unaccounted for who had died, but who had no one to pass it on to. With that final one hundred thousand that was left over, I set up a trust fund for Millie to access when she turned eighteen, all in the name of her war-hero grandfather, Damon Hardy.

But more important than that, more important

than anything else for me, was that the memory of my deceased wife wasn't tarnished. Claire's dying wish, to provide a safety net for her beloved niece, was restored.

With an agreement from Ben, I set-up a trust fund for Alannah, my niece, in the memory of my wife. That was what she left in her will. That's what she wanted to do with the money she left behind. Ben and I became co-signatories, meaning the money could only be accessed with agreement from both of us. After the events of the last two weeks, I couldn't imagine that Ben would ever come to me for money before Alannah turned eighteen.

"You made me leave that money on the park bench." Chase pointed his finger in my direction. "You made me lose the million."

I raised my eyebrows.

And he lowered his finger.

"I didn't make you do anything, Chase. What I did was save your daughter. I saved a five-year-old girl from being killed. Haven't you seen the news? The last two kidnappings in Florida have ended up with missing money and dead kids. We didn't have that here. Sure, you're missing your money, but what's money when you have your child back?"

He looked perplexed, because he knew I was right.

The last two kidnappings handled by the FBI in Florida had become public after they failed to secure the child, while still losing the money. That wasn't going to happen in Chicago. Not in my city. I made sure of it.

"You planned this," Chase whispered. "You ripped me off. I got a phone call today from one of the guys in the investment group who was bragging that he had my money. He had it all back. He said that I 'donated' it to him."

Well, they weren't supposed to do that, but then, if I was dealing with a man like Chase Martin, I would've called him as well. I would have laughed in his face and let him know that I got the better of him. It was the least that he deserved. In truth he deserved jail, and who knows, perhaps it wouldn't be long before that caught up with him as well. But for now, he had his daughter and his freedom and for that, he should have been thankful, no matter what the financial cost.

"You left the money in the park, Chase. I don't know what happened to it after we left. You made the decision to save your daughter, which was the right decision." I stood up straight. "I didn't see anyone take that money, and nor did you. We don't know who took your money. It could've been a homeless guy, for all we know. We were a mile down the road before anyone would've even seen that bag."

"That's not true." Chase shook his head, still coming to terms with the fact that he had been beaten. "You ripped me off. Millie told me that she had been with Damon the whole time I thought she

243

was missing, just hanging out, watching movies. She said Damon left her alone to watch television sometimes, and then would come back with the best doughnuts. I didn't believe her at first, I thought she must've been dreaming about it, but then she mentioned Casey. Someone had to get Millie from the warehouse to the park, and that someone had to be you."

"You can't prove anything." I smiled and raised my hands. "But unfortunately for you, I can, if I feel like it. Things have been a bit slow here this week and I have a lot of paperwork the FBI would like to look over, anonymously left with me, relating to some financial irregularities. There are some links missing, but nothing that a good private investigator couldn't find out. I've enjoyed a few quiet days, but it would be good to get my teeth stuck into some proper investigative work next week, if no new cases turn up, that is."

Chase shook his head again, and paced the floor, clearly beaten. "You're a piece of work, Jack."

"Thank you." I smiled. "How is Millie?"

He stared at me, his jaw clenched, but then he relaxed.

"I love that girl. More than anything. This whole drama has made me realize that she should be the main girl in my life. She always should've been my main girl. Ruby's moved to California now, so I can finally focus on Millie. It's best for her to spend the most time with her mother, but when Millie needs me, I'll be there." He looked to the floor. "I couldn't dream of losing her. She's… she's an angel. Just like Damon used to say."

"I'm glad she got through this without any mental scars. She wouldn't even know that anything went wrong."

"She told Tanya that I asked Damon to look after her and that she got to spend some time by herself in a warehouse. Tanya went off at me." He shrugged. "Said it was my fault. That I shouldn't have asked Damon to care for her while I was supposed to be looking after her."

"Looks like everyone's a winner."

"I'm not. I lost a million dollars." He snapped back. For a moment, I thought he had grown a heart, but the mere mention of money snapped him back. "I was the loser in this whole scenario. And I don't like losing."

"Can't win everything," I shrugged. "Sometimes losing makes you stronger. And by the sounds of it, you have started to understand how important Millie is to you."

"Don't lecture me." He raised his finger again, gritting his teeth. "How could you justify ripping off your clients?"

At first I thought he was joking, that he was employing a little sarcasm for comedic effect, and he was finding it within himself to laugh at his own misfortune.

But then I realized that he was serious.

He couldn't see the double standard or the irony. That there really was a one-way moral mirror with Chase Martin that reflected nothing of his ill deeds back towards him. I tried to lay it out for him.

"You tell me, Chase."

His face went white. "I don't…"

"Tell me how does it feel, Chase?" I took a step towards him. "How does it feel to have your hard earned money disappear, not that yours is hard earned, knowing that you have no legal recourse? Do you feel helpless? Weak and beaten?" I stepped into his personal space. "Helpless like you made all those other people feel when you ripped them off?"

"Of course, I feel helpless." As he said the statement, his voice trailed off, no doubt finally understanding the extreme hypocrisy in it. "Nobody deserves to be ripped off."

"Well, Chase." I walked across the room and opened the door for him to leave. "As you repeated often, that's the game we all play."

THE END

AUTHOR'S NOTE:

Thank you for reading The Hostage. I hope you enjoyed the twists and turns of this story.

Thank you to all the people that made this story happen. Writing is about drawing from experience, and the characters in this book have elements of the people I've met throughout life. No matter how much I disagree with them, I love listening to other ideas and outlooks on life. Not many people have it all figured out, and we can all learn a little bit from each other.

If you enjoyed this book, please leave a review.

You can find my website at: peteromahoney.com

And if you wish, you can contact me at: peter@peteromahoney.com

Take care,
Peter O'Mahoney

ALSO BY PETER O'MAHONEY

In the Jack Valentine Mystery Series:

Gates of Power
The Shooter
The Thief
The Witness

*****

In the Tex Hunter Legal Thriller series:

Power and Justice
Faith and Justice
Corrupt Justice
Deadly Justice
Saving Justice
Natural Justice
Freedom and Justice
Losing Justice
Failing Justice

*****

In the Joe Hennessy Legal Thriller series:

The Southern Lawyer
The Southern Criminal
The Southern Killer

Printed in Great Britain
by Amazon

32575437R00144